1

Dedication

This book is dedicated to my family, friends, and Hideaki Sorachi. Thank you for your encouragement, support, and inspiration.

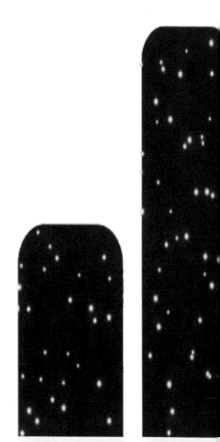

1 Can You Keep a Promise?

The room was dark, with the only source of light being a dimly lit lamp.

In the room, a trio of rugged men seated anxiously at a desk.

Across from them, a slender man dressed in blacks and grays and a crow-like mask covering his face's upper half.

"We'll ask one more time." One of the three men barked.

"Can we trust you to carry out this mission?"

The shaded man relaxing in his seat with arms stretched behind his head, chuckled.

"For the last time, I'm sure I can help assist those already doomed by fate."

The men exchanged looks and begrudgingly handed the paper to the masked man.

"We'll see how you do within a month." One of the men said sighing.

Carelessly skimming the paper, the man couldn't help but think; *how hard can this mission be?*

*

The bell rang faintly to signal the start of lunch. The hallway usually quiet with just whispers, and the faint sound of IV drips, now filled with the loud chatter of a variety of different conversations buzzing around the cafeteria.

Three children sat in a row at the left end of the cafeteria. One with her head down, focused on drawing, one smiling as he bit into one of his rare treats from his Auntie, and one staring out the window in a daze.

Suddenly the girls' attention was grabbed by the boy, offering her a quarter of his sandwich.

Just finishing her masterpiece, the other girl turned her head around, revealing a piece of crust in her mouth.

"No, thank you." The girl quickly turned her attention back to the window.

"C'mon!" The boy protested.

"You haven't eaten anything yet!"

The girl keeping her attention on the window, gave an uninterested nod.

"By the way," the other girl said, wiping away eraser shavings on her drawing.

"Did you hear that there's a new doctor in our unit?" The boy turned curiously.

 "Another one? Isn't this the third already?"

The girl gave a nod.

"I heard it's because they can't take the job."

"The job?" The girl took her attention away from the window curiously.

"Wow, how do you know all of this, 247?" The boy asked, intrigued.

"Well," the girl started as a guard towered over them.

"Lunch is over; get back to your rooms now." She glared.

The boy quickly handed the girl the rest of his sandwich and smiled up at the guard.

"Thank you; I didn't hear the bell!"

"Go!" The guard barked.

*

Upon entering her room, the girl looked down at the sandwich, nervously glancing towards the door, then back at her sandwich. As she opened her mouth, she heard a knock and quickly stuffed the sandwich in her gown, panicked.

However, she heard the door of the room next to hers open instead and sighed in relief.

She suddenly remembered what 247 had said earlier about there being a new doctor in their unit as she took a bite.

I hope he isn't scared of us this time. She thought.

*

"Almost done..." The man looked at the boy, who had his eyes tightly shut as his blood was being drawn.

"There we go." The man tapped his arm to let him know it was over.

"Usually, it hurts, but it didn't hurt now!" The boy opening his eyes, smiled.

"Ah." The man gave a nodding smile as he labeled the tubes.

"What's your name?" The boy questioned as he swung his legs.

"Hm?" The man looked up after pasting on the last label.

"Your name?" The boy asked again, curiously.

"Ah, my name." The man smiled.

"You can just call me Reaper, I guess."

The boy looked at him in confusion.

"That's your real name?"

"Well," the man began.

"Sorry, Mr. Reaper, I hope that wasn't rude." The boy said quickly.

"You're fine." The man chuckled.

"Also…" The boy started again.

"Why are you wearing that mask?" He questioned.

"Oh, the mask," the man frowned.

"I like to think it looks cool, I guess." He chuckled to himself.

"Oh, ok!" The boy was satisfied with the answer.

"I'll be right back...I have to go test these." The man picking up the tray of tubes began to walk towards the door.

"Ok!" The boy said as he waved.

*

"Damn." The man sighed, turning onto his back.

"These beds are uncomfortable as hell." He frowned at the ceiling.

Suddenly, he thought about earlier that day with his assignment. He then let out a sigh.

That kid isn't going to make it. He rolled onto his side, closed his eyes, and drifted off to sleep.

*

"Oh! Good morning, Mr. Reaper!"

The man turned around and met eyes with his assignment.

"Ah." The man smiled.

"Morning, 245," he said, turning away towards the employee's table.

"245!" A voice cried out.

The boy turned face to face with his friend.

"Oh, 247!" He smiled.

"Is that him?" She asked, looking in The Reapers' direction.

"Hm?" The boy cocked his head.

He then realized that she meant their new doctor.

"Oh, yeah, that's him!" He smiled.

"He said his name is Reaper!" He laughed.

"Reaper-"

The girl was suddenly interrupted, towered by a figure.

"Sit down; this isn't story time!" The guard barked. The two quickly sped walked back to their table.

"Where's 246?" The boy looked up after chewing a spoonful of his cereal.

"Maybe she's getting blood work?" The girl shrugged.

*

"Do you think we're stupid?"

There was silence.

"Oi, brat!" He angrily shouted.

"Well," he said with a frustrated sigh.

"I hope that sandwich was good because, as punishment, we will be taking away your lunch hours," he grinned.

"That'll teach you." The man snarled as he walked out.

The girl, too shocked to process the scolding or worry much for the punishment, just looked helplessly towards the window.

*

"Your boy is on the 'to die' list." A co-worker said, turning to The Reaper.

"The injections don't seem to be doing much of anything; therefore, he has been deemed useless."

"Ah." The Reaper responded while looking at the bulletin squinting.

"Any ideas on how you'll tell a child such a thing?" The man asked The Reaper, letting out a sigh.

"This place pities not even the innocence of a child." He continued.

The Reaper turned his attention towards the man.

"It sure is a shame," he smiled quietly.

"Man…" He whispered.

"How could I break the news to such a puppy-eyed boy?"

The man sighed.

"Well, that would be up to you, I suppose."

"Yeah, but…" The Reaper began.

"A killer questioning how to kill his prey?" The man chuckled as he walked away.

The Reaper glared, then let out a long sigh.

*

"Wow, not even a flinch." The Reaper chuckled.

"I told you I'm not scared anymore, Mr. Reaper!" The boy smiled up at him.

That warm smile. Those innocent eyes, so full of life. None of the assignments he's ever had have involved the duty of having to kill a child.

He had to let him know. He couldn't let the boy go with no idea what was happening.

"Have you-" the Reaper paused.

"Hm?" The boy turned his attention towards the man.

"Humans, we can't live forever, you know." The room suddenly filled with a dreadful silence.

"I know." The boy quietly answered.

"Some deserve to live longer lives, and yet, inevitably, some die young, cruel deaths." The Reaper said as he looked out the window.

The boy gave a silent nod.

"245," The Reaper began.

"I've been told I was too weak for my medicine." The boy muttered quietly. "Am I-" he looked up at the Reaper, who still had his attention focused on the window. "Am I... dying?"

The Reaper turned slowly to face the boy.

"Sometimes, life just sucks." He gave a try-hard smile.

The boy nodded slowly.

"Mr. Reaper?"

"Mm?"

"Can you be the one to kill me?"

The room once more fell quiet.

"Ah, I meant, please." The boy gave a slight smile.

The Reaper looked around the room for answers.

Does a boy like this? A boy like this doesn't deserve to die at the blood-stained hands of a cold, calculated killer such as himself.

However, the boy had requested this. The boy needed some sort of closure that only he, The Reaper knew how to provide.

The man smiled softly as he weakly walked towards the drawer containing the needle.

This boy doesn't deserve to die. He told himself repeatedly in his head like a broken record.

He flicked the needle a couple of times.

The Reaper studied himself in the mirror for a moment.

The last thing the boy deserved to see was a crow dirtied by the sins he's carried with that mask.

He gently placed the needle down as he began to remove his mask.

The Reaper looked at himself once more and gave himself a slight nod of reassurance as he gently picked the needle back up.

The boy facing the door of the room next to him, turned back around.

"Oh!" He said, amazed.

"You took your mask off!" He laughed.

The man couldn't help but stare for a good second as this boy laughed in the presence of death.

A death they both knew he didn't deserve.

"It was getting in the way." The Reaper chuckled.

"By the way," the boy began quietly.

"Mr. Reaper, can you keep a promise?"

The Reaper once more became stunned by the boy and his pure innocence.

A promise? He thought.

"Well, they certainly shouldn't be taken lightly."

"But, can you keep one?" The boy repeated himself.

The Reaper hesitantly opened his mouth.

"Well, it really depends-"

"There's a girl next door." The boy pointed towards the door he'd been facing.

"Her name," he paused.

"Her name is 246." The boy looked up to make sure the Reaper was still following along.

"246." The Reaper repeated back.

"She's very quiet; nobody, not even the doctors, know about her past." He paused.

"She's my best friend," he said, as he began to tear up.

The Reaper quickly grabbed a tissue and began dabbing the boy's face, almost instinctively.

"Can you...will you protect her?"

The Reaper met eyes with the boy.

The boy staring hopefully into the eyes of death.

The Reaper reached for the needle. He gave a smile and raised his pinky towards the boy.

"I promise." He smiled as he injected the needle into the boy's arm.

He laid the limp boy softly down onto the table, resting his arm.

You didn't even flinch. The Reaper thought to himself.

Tears streamed down his face.

2 Escape

"245?" There was a knock. The Reaper froze for a second.

Then he realized the knock was coming from the room next door.

That must be 246. The man thought to himself as he opened the door.

The man looked down, met with the big eyes of a tiny girl.

"246, huh?"

The girl jumped a bit at the sound of her name.

"Y-yes..." she whispered.

"It's a pleasure to meet you finally." He smiled.

"If you'd like, you can call me Rick."

"Rick..." The girl repeated back.

"Yep!" The man smiled once more.

The girl gave a slight nod as she held her hands to her chest.

"Why don't we have a seat?"

Before she could respond, Rick lifted her and placed her carefully on top of the table.

"There we go." He then noticed the girl looking down steadily.

"Not the type of striking up a conversation, huh?" He chuckled.

She kept looking down.

"Well," Rick began.

"Why don't we start with blood work."

The girl looked up.

"I don't like needles..." She whispered, then winced presumably at the thought of a needle.

"Hm," Rick said as he looked around the room studying it.

"Well," he clapped his hands together.

"Let's make a deal!" He smiled.

"Huh?" The girl looked up.

"If you let me draw your blood this once with a boring band-aid, tomorrow, I'll bring in special band-aids, just for you!"

The girl looked up, amazed.

"Really?"

"Really!" He nodded.

"C-can they be bunnies?" She looked hopeful.

"Bunnies, huh?" He thought for a second.

"Alright! I'll try my best!" He smiled.

The girl gave a nod and smile.

"Ok then! hold out your arm for me, please."

He looked and saw her carefully raising her arm towards him.

"Good girl..." He whispered.

"On the count of three, follow my finger around the room, please."

She raised her head and began following his finger.

"Done!" He smiled as he finished blotting, then putting the band-aid on the spot where the needle had been.

The girl looked at him, amazed.

"That didn't hurt!" She exclaimed excitedly.

Rick sheepishly rubbed the back of his head.

"I'm glad to hear that!" He smiled.

"I can't wait to tell 245!" She smiled happily.

Rick froze.

"Uh... yeah!" He looked away.

"Oh! It's lunchtime now!" She cried, hopping down from the table.

Rick looked around helplessly. He didn't have the energy or the mentality to tell her that her best friend was now dead.

Especially because of him.

As the girl opened the door, they heard a woman screaming and hysterically crying.

"YOU KILLED MY BOY!"

"YOU KNEW OUR DEAL, AND YET-"

Rick quickly grabbed the child's shoulders and carefully pulled her back into the room.

"It's probably not safe out there..."

As he held her shoulders, he felt them bobbing up and down.

That's when he heard a sniffle.

"246?"

"Hey-"

"That was 245's Aunt…" She whispered.

She then broke out into full sobs.

"Is he…" She began with breaks in her sobs, raising her head to look up at Rick.

"I'm afraid," he began as he felt a tiny body grip onto him.

246 began sobbing into him.

Rick glanced out the peephole.

Men were carrying the corpse of the child that he had killed.

This is the first time in forever since he had felt so guilty, and so dirty for committing a murder.

But all he could do now was to protect the girl, the victim's best friend; he had to keep the promise.

He began stroking her hair gently as he let her fully embrace him.

*

It's 3 am, and I'm here searching for how to draw a bunny. Rick scratched his head, annoyed.

After he left 246, he immediately went to a pharmacy searching for what he thought would be a no brainer. *How the hell do they not sell bunny band-aids?* He sighed as he carefully drew the ears on the last bunny.

There. He sighed.

"This place..." He whispered to himself.

We need to get the hell out of here. He flicked the lights off and drifted off to sleep.

*

As he walked, he let out a big yawn, stretching his arms. He had not gotten much sleep after all.

"Oi."

He turned, looking to see who was talking to him.

"Huh?" He responded as he let out another yawn.

"You're not in this department today."

Rick looked around.

"I think you have the wrong person-"

"No-" The other man began.

"You've been too soft with these experiments,

Therefore, you've been moved to the adult's department."

Before he could protest, the man sneered.

"Hugging those things dirties your pretty white coat, you know." He laughed, walking away.

Rick stood there stunned, but he didn't have time to get angry and start a fight.

He began running down the hall, not stopping until he reached the bulletin.

He skimmed through the numbers on the 'to die' list.

That's when his heart dropped.

He noticed that '246' was on the list.

No. He thought to himself in utter disbelief.

Her abilities were starting to kick in; she bloomed to be what they would refer to as a successful experiment. *So why. Why...?*

But he had no time to think; he thought about the plan he hatched up but threw to the side not thinking that this would happen.

He had to hurry. They had to escape.

He began running once more.

*

"Well, kid," the doctor began.

"You know, what happens when little brats don't behave here, don't you?" He smirked.

"I don't know..." The girl whispered.

"That was a rhetorical question, dummy." The man then laughed.

"Then again, you probably don't know how to write your own name." He snickered.

The girl sat there quietly.

What happened to the nice man, Rick, he forgot to keep his promise? They always do... She began to tear up.

"Ah, you're crying!?" The doctor snapped.

"There'll be no room for tears where you're going now, sweetheart."

He flicked the needle *once.*

"More like screaming of the damned." He laughed.

Twice.

He rose the needle in her direction.

"Demons like you should've stayed right in hell!"

Three.

She looked up, horrified as she saw the needle coming right at her, panicked; she screamed, closing her eyes and by reflex, swatted the needle away.

There was silence.

One.

She breathed heavily.

Two.

She began to open her eyes.

Three.

She looked down to see a body lying on the floor.

Horrified, she began sobbing uncontrollably.

It was an accident. She just hated needles. She was scared because of the screaming. She didn't mean to. She didn't want to.

Suddenly, the door opened.

She jumped up, then noticed it was the doctor from yesterday.

She sobbed even wilder than before and pointed towards the body.

"I didn't mean to!" She was hysterical.

He couldn't even begin to care about the scene.

She was safe. She was alive. And that's all that mattered.

"246." He grabbed her by the shoulders.

"We need to get out of here and fast." "Do you trust me?" He looked her in the eyes.

The girl couldn't comprehend what was happening, but she gave a nod.

"Good girl." He said, picking her up and carrying her under his arm.

He began to run.

He ran into a medicine cart, but that didn't stop him.

He kept running as if his life depended on it.

With her tucked under his arm, he ran like hell.

He noticed the door towards the end of the hall.

Freedom. He thought.

He hadn't looked back once but heard the alarms going off.

Too late. He thought.

They had successfully made it outside before the lockdown began.

Despite being outside, he wouldn't dare risk it, so he kept running as fast as possible.

He then turned a corner and noticed a cab.

He banged on the window, startling the driver inside.

The driver rolled down his window.

"I could've choked on my sandwich!" He cried.

Unfazed, Rick opened the door, quickly put 246 inside, then got in himself.

"Where to?" The driver grumbled.

"I don't care; take us to any town you can think of." He breathed heavily.

"Oh, don't worry, buddy, I've got just the place." He laughed.

"Wait," he paused.

"Just go!" Rick cried.

The driver quickly put the car in drive and drove off.

"Cash or credit?" He asked impatiently.

"Cash." Rick sighed, still out of breath.

He then glanced down, momentarily forgetting about the girl accompanying him on their escape.

"246..." He took his coat off, wrapping it around the girl.

He smiled, collecting his breath.

"We made it." He laughed.

No response.

"246?" He stared down at the girl.

"246-"

"It's winter?" She questioned.

"Ah, well, actually fall just began." He said, brushing his hand through her hair.

"It's cold." She looked up at him.

"Yeah, it is pretty chilly." He chuckled. She stared at him for a long second.

"Hey." She tugged his arm.

"Hm?" He looked back down towards her.

"Are we…" She whispered.

"…Free?" She asked as she kept her gaze on him.

Rick looked out the window on the other side.

"I sure hope so." He smiled.

"Also," she began.

"Hm?" He looked over.

"Did you get my bunny band-aids?" She asked, with a hint of hope.

Kids… He thought to himself, amused.

"As a matter of fact, yes, I did!" He dug into his pants pocket and pulled out three band-aids with bunnies drawn onto them.

The girl's eyes twinkled.

"You kept your promise!" She beamed.

He chuckled.

I sure did. He thought to himself as he began to nod off.

3 Flowers

The car came to a jolting stop.

"Huh?" Rick lifted his head lethargically.

"This is as far as I'll go." The taxi driver said.

"Alright," Rick said, rubbing his eyes.

"How much?"

"A hundred and twenty."

"Christ…"

Rick looked down at the girl who, to his surprise, was still awake.

"Give me a sec." Rick began feeling his pockets for his wallet.

"Eh…?" Rick kept feeling his pockets anxiously.

"Don't tell me…"The driver mumbled.

The girl suddenly tapped him.

"Huh?" He glanced down.

"Your wallet fell out when you gave me the Band-Aids." She informed him.

There was a sigh of relief from both men.

"Thanks a lot," Rick said, begrudgingly handing over a hundred and twenty.

"By the way," the driver began.

"There aren't any hotels within this town, but the people are pretty easygoing!" He laughed.

"Hey!" Rick cried out.

"W-wait...!"

However, the driver sped off.

"Son of a-" Rick once again noticed the girl accompanying him. *I guess I'll have to work on that.* He let out a sigh.

"Oi," he began.

"Did you even get any sleep?"

The girl looked around, then shook her head silently.

"I was too scared."

"Huh?"

"They won't find us, will they?" She asked.

He froze for a minute. He didn't know whether there was a search party out looking for them or not. But then again, with the Lab's ties to the government, they most likely wouldn't want to cause a public outcry and make both the Labs and the Government look bad.

"I-" He began as he turned and saw two men with flashlights.

There wasn't time to waste. Whether they were with the Labs or not, he wasn't willing to wait around to find out.

He grabbed the girl and ran into an alley.

"Rick-" The girl began but was silenced by a hand.

"Just relax," he told her.

Hiding behind a garbage can was an old trick in the book, but it might've just worked if they were quiet. About twenty minutes passed, and another wave of exhaustion had hit them both; suddenly, they were out.

*

"Hello?"

"Hello...?"

The man began stirring. He could barely open his eyes, but he was met with a woman standing above them when he did.

"Huh?" Rick answered sluggishly.

"Ah, you're finally awake." The lady began.

"Mm." Rick then looked around and noticed the girl wasn't anywhere to be found. Fully alert now, he looked around once more.

"Where is-"

"That girl..." The lady began.

"So, you've seen her?" He looked up at her and sighed in relief.

"Yes," the lady began.

"She's on my couch," she then paused.

"What is your relation to her?" She asked cautiously.

Eh? Rick froze.

He only met her a couple of days ago, like hell, he would know. But then again, he was tied to her by a promise. At least, for now, his job and focus were to protect her.

"Well-" He began.

"You don't strike me as a creep." She said, cutting him off.

What. What the hell did this lady say? Why would the word creep come into play? Did she really find him creepy?

"Huh!?" He looked up, alarmed.

"Of course not!" He shouted angrily.

"What did she even tell you!?"

"Oh!" The lady smiled. "That was just my evaluation." She laughed.

What the hell kind of...

"She had spoken something about the two of you running away."

"That kid-" He stood up, stretching his back sorely.

"I don't know what she told you, and I apologize-" Rick began.

"But I really need to keep an eye on this kid." He stated firmly.

"Would you like to come in?" The lady asked.

He looked around cluelessly.

The lady pointed to the building next to them.

"That's my shop." She smiled.

"Sena's Flowers."

"Are you Sena?" He questioned, looking at the sign.

"Yep! This is a self-made business!" She beamed.

"Follow me," she said, opening the door.

"Your-" She began, and then paused.

"The girl," she started again.

"She's up these stairs." She said, smiling.

Rick climbed the spiral creaky wooden staircase leading up to a small entranceway met with a door. He opened the door and saw the girl sitting on the couch watching TV.

"24-" He paused.

"Kid..." He began as he quickly walked over to the couch.

"Rick!" She smiled, looking up at him.

"Good morning!" She beamed.

"Kid," he began.

"Hm?" She turned her attention back to him.

"You shouldn't have put this nice lady through all of this trouble," he began.

"But..." The girl began in protest.

"She offered me to come in..." She said, looking down steadily.

"Ah," The woman walked over.

"I was throwing my trash out and noticed you and your girl."

"She was awake at the time and looked scared." She paused.

"She recoiled, so I took a step back."

"But," she began giggling.

"Her stomach grumbled, so I offered her food."

No kid could pass the food test. Rick thought.

"After I fed her, I asked her who she was with." She looked at Rick.

"She told me you two were running from someone or something." She frowned.

"Ah yeah," he said, stretching his arms up.

"Kids tend to say the darndest things, huh?" He paused.

"Anyway, I really appreciate that you are feeding her, but I'm afraid we have to dine and dash."

"C'mon, kid."

"But-" The lady began.

"Rick," the girl looked up at him.

"If you're telling me you weren't up to something, then why would you be laying behind my trash can?" She looked at him.

"Well-" Rick scratched the back of his head.

"Please, just have a cup of coffee and talk." She walked over to him.

"I'm a florist, not a cop." She smiled, grabbing his hand.

Rick looked around helplessly and let out a sigh.

"Coffee sounds nice." He looked over at the girl, who was glued to the television.

*

"So, you worked at a science lab," she began.

"Basically," he paused, sipping his coffee.

"I don't know if you quaint townsfolk know of an 'Experiment Labs' or not, but." He said, glancing into his cup.

"No, I honestly haven't heard of it." She frowned.

"Well, I guess that's a good thing for you." He chuckled.

"It's a pretty corrupt place," he began.

"Let's just say humans are the test subjects."

"What?" She asked, with a hint of alarm.

"It's not pretty," he said, looking down steadily.

"Basically, I wanted to get us out of there." He met eyes with the curious woman.

"Were you-" Sena began.

"Both test subjects?" She looked at the girl and back at him.

The girl looked away quickly, back towards the TV.

"No, just her." He answered quietly.

"Then what were you-"

"I was her doctor." He responded quickly.

"Wow," Sena said, stunned.

There was a moment of silence, with only noise from the TV in the background.

"Do you have anywhere to stay?" Sena asked, looking down steadily at her cup.

"Not really."

"Do you-" She looked up at him but quickly looked away once more.

"Need...somewhere?"

"Huh?" Rick looked at her in confusion.

"Well," she began.

"Until whenever you think you two are in the clear, you're welcome to use this apartment."

"I appreciate it, but-" Rick started.

"Where else would you go?" She began, looking up at him.

Rick looked around.

"Don't you live here, though?" He asked, scratching his head.

"Actually-" Sena began.

"I used to rent this apartment out to my friend, but when her dad got sick, she had to move back home."

She looked at the floor.

"There aren't any hotels in this town, you know."

Rick glanced at the girl, back to his cup, and finally back to Sena.

"Rent?"

"Hm?" She looked up.

"How much did your friend pay?" He paused.

"I can pay that, but for two."

"Does two-hundred a month sound reasonable?" She looked up, hopefully.

"That's it?" He looked at her, stunned.

"I'm really not the best with pricing." She laughed.

Rick looked at the girl who was now looking at him with somewhat hopeful eyes.

"I'll-" He then paused.

"We'll take it." He said, sighing in relief.

The girl beamed happily, and Sena clapped her hands together.

"Wonderful!" She smiled.

"I'll give you the first payment when I get around to an ATM." He said, getting up.

"Give us a tour?" He smiled.

4 Maru

It had been a few nights since Rick begrudgingly agreed to house him and the girl in Sena's Flowers. It was a small space, which was fine since it was just the two of them.

The girl had been strong in her pleas to claim the bedroom; however, Rick wasn't having it.

"The couch is plenty big for you." He would tell her.

She would pout, yet it was all in vain. After numerous failed attempts, she gave up.

One night, the two were having dinner that Sena had brought over from the local cafe.

As Sena was setting the table, she pulled Rick to the side.

"Hey," she began.

"Yes?" Rick looked at her.

"Does she really not have a name?"

Rick glanced at the girl and back to Sena.

"Not really..." He mumbled.

245's words proved to be true. The girl's papers ended up not having much information on her background, thus no name.

"Aren't you tired of calling her 'kid,' though?" Sena questioned.

"Listen-" Rick huffed.

"What do you suggest I do then?" He asked.

"Well," Sena began with a big smile.

Rick didn't like where this was going. Whenever Sena smiled like that, it meant she was up to something. It irked him.

"Have you ever had a pet?"

He looked at her.

"What-"

"Even if you haven't, there's always a thrill to giving something or someone a name!" She beamed.

Rick turned to look at the girl, who was blissfully unaware in food heaven. He sighed.

"Do you have any ideas?"

Sena frowned.

"But she's your-" She paused

quickly.

Rick raised an eyebrow.

"She's my...?"

"It's only right if you name her." She looked at him.

"Oh, geez, I have to get home!" She cried.

Rick looked around helplessly as Sena waved goodbye to him and patted the girl on the head. He waved back weakly.

As Sena left, he walked back over to the table and sat down.

"Hey-" He began.

"Mm?" The girl looked up with a face full of sauce.

Rick chuckled as he grabbed a napkin.

"You-" He began.

"You don't have a name that you're hiding from us now, hm?" He began wiping the girl's mouth.

The girl looked down.

"No." She mumbled.

"Ah."

That was all that Rick could

manage.

The girl yawned.

"Tired?"

"Mm." The girl nodded.

"Why don't we get you to bed then?" Rick smiled as he helped her down from the chair.

They walked over to the couch, and the girl plopped down.

"Guess the pasta wore you out, huh?" He questioned, chuckling in amusement.

"Mm." The girl looked at him for a second, then looked away.

"Night, Rick." She smiled gently.

"Goodnight." He said as he pulled the blanket over her and gave her a quick pat on the head.

*

Rick took out a notepad and placed it down on his desk.

Guess this kid isn't naming herself. He sighed.

He opened his phone up to the search engine.

"Alright." He began typing in the only possible question he could think of.

'Names for girls.' He scratched his head and pressed the first website.

'Annabelle,' he scrolled. 'Ashley.'

He scrolled again. None of these names sounded right.

He got to L. 'Lee, Lindsay, Lori.' Nope.

He then went down to M.

He noticed the section where it told what the names meant.

"That would've helped a lot before." He grumbled.

'Mari' nope.

'Maru.'

He paused.

'Maru is a great feminine name, meaning gentle.' The site read.

He then thought back to earlier when she smiled. The girl had a cute yet gentle smile.

"Why not..." He chuckled.

"I guess Maru best suits her." He yawned, laying his head down in his arms.

*

"Rick, Rick, Rick?"

"Mmm...?" He began stirring.

"Wh- Huh?"

"I told you I should've taken the bed!" The girl cried.

Rick looked at the clock. '8:52'.

Damn it. He fell asleep at his desk and overslept.

"What do you want for breakfast, Maru?" He asked, scratching his back as he got up and stretched.

The girl just looked at him.

"Who are you talking to?" She asked.

"I'm talking to y-"

"Oh!" He exclaimed.

The girl kept looking at him, puzzled. "Don't be silly, Maru."

She still didn't get it.

"Maru-" He laughed nervously.

Nothing.

"Do you like that name?" He asked.

"Hm?" She looked at him.

"I hope so, because that's your name now, Maru." He said, ruffling her hair.

She quickly looked up at him.

"Really!?" She exclaimed.

"As long as you like it, why not?" He laughed.

Sena was right. It was much easier to say 'Maru, please pass the milk' rather than 'hey kid, pass it over here.' Plus, Maru enjoyed her name, so he was relieved.

*

"Maru, hm?" Sena questioned as she looked at her.

Maru nodded excitedly.

"Well, I think that name suits you perfectly." She smiled, looking over at Rick, who in return gave a confident nod.

5 Metamorphosis

There was a knock.

"Come in." Rick tilted his head towards the door.

Nothing.

"Oi, Sena, I said come in!" He spoke up louder.

However, the door opened to Rick's surprise. It wasn't Sena; rather, it was another lady. This lady was tall with broad shoulders. Dressed in a white blouse, with a long blue skirt. She had long red hair tied in a messy bun resembling a ponytail.

Rick stared for a solid second. His vision wasn't the best; in fact, he probably needed glasses soon, but this was not his landlady.

"Um…" The lady looked around.

"Don't mind me, I guess. I'm just here to get a few more of my things…" She mumbled as she walked over to the kitchen.

Rick was floored. Was she in the right home? Was she an intruder? Would she pounce any second?

Then it hit him.

Before he and Maru moved in, Sena had mentioned a friend who had previously lived in their home.

"Are you-" He began.

"Did you," He rephrased.

"You used to live here?"

The lady looked up from her box.

"Yeah." She looked around.

"I see you did some redecorating." She smiled.

"How's your dad?"

"Sena mentioned you had to leave because he was sick."

The lady looked away quickly.

"He-" she bit her lip.

"He passed."

"Oh, I'm s-"

"Anyway," the lady began.

"Where's Sena?"

Rick scratched his head.

"She's out with my kid."

"Maru?" The lady suddenly smiled.

Rick looked up quickly.

"I was hoping to meet her today, but I'm afraid I have things to get done today." She sighed.

 "Well, they should be coming home soon-"

"I really have to get going." She paused, then began again.

"I'm glad I didn't come back to an empty house." The lady smiled softly.

"By the way, the name's Abbey."

"Ah, Rick." He said, smiling as he introduced himself.

"Later." Abbey walked out, carrying a box.

Rick slumped back in his chair. *Where the heck are those two?* He sighed.

*

"We're home!"

Rick walked out of his bedroom, greeted by Maru, Sena, and at least a dozen shopping bags.

"Ah, welcome home." He greeted, patting Maru's head.

"Hey, Rick," Sena began.

"Hm?"

She motioned him towards the kitchenette.

"What's up?" He leaned against the counter.

"I wanted your permission-" She then paused.

"Are you ok?"

Rick looked at her, confused.

"Why wouldn't I be?" He asked.

"Well, you're blinking an awful lot."

"Ah," Rick smirked.

"What?" Sena asked.

"It's nothing." He looked at the floor, then quickly back at Sena.

"I just can't see... that's all."

Sena frowned.

"Do you think you need glasses?"

"Well-" Rick began.

Sena held up her hand. "How many fingers?" She asked.

Rick sighed. "We're not in kindergarten-"

"How many?" Sena demanded, cutting him off.

"Technically four, since your thumb doesn't count."

"I've never heard about that before," Sena said, laughing.

Rick brushed his hair back.

"We're getting off-topic here; what were you going to ask earlier?"

"Oh!" Sena smiled as he reminded her.

"Maru needs a haircut." She smiled.

Rick frowned, puzzled.

"Why didn't you get one while you were out for all that while?" He asked.

Sena looked towards Maru.

"For starters," she said, looking back to him.

"I wanted your permission; plus, she wants you to be there."

Rick sighed. He then thought for a moment. In the chance anyone from Experiment Labs was looking for them, a haircut might serve the purpose of a disguise.

"Getting a haircut doesn't sound like a bad idea." He smiled over at Maru.

She did look like she desperately needed a haircut. It was all-around long, albeit it being straight, it was messy. There was also that one long strand of hair in the middle of her face down to her cheek.

"Yay!" Maru beamed as she grabbed his hand and pulled him out the door.

Sena followed behind, giggling.

*

"How does she want it cut?" The barber questioned, turning to Sena and Rick.

Rick, who was nose deep in a magazine, looked up.

"Tell him what you want, Maru." He said, looking back down.

"Rick-" Sena began.

"What? It's her hair!" He huffed.

"I don't know, does neck length sound reasonable?"
He said, looking at a poster that had 'neck length'
hairstyles on it.

"She just needs it out of her face."

Maru nodded.

"That's what you want?" Sena questioned the girl.

Maru gave a thumbs up.

"Okay!" Sena smiled, giving a thumbs-up back.

*

"And done." The barber said, spinning the chair
around towards the adults.

Rick looked up.

She looked like an entirely new kid. Her hair was now
neck length, with 'M' shaped bangs. He couldn't help
but smile as he saw the girl beaming.

"You look so adorable!" Sena cried, hugging her.

Rick walked over, patting the girl on the head.

"I like it." He smiled.

Maru beamed up at them.

*

As Rick was paying, Sena looked out the door.

"Oh!" She exclaimed.

Rick grabbed the change and thanked the barber.

"What's up?" He turned towards her.

"There's a glasses shop across the street." She smiled, pointing.

"Ah, well-" Rick began hesitantly.

"What's wrong?" Sena frowned.

"You said you needed glasses."

"I did." He said, opening the door.

"Just not today."

Sena grabbed him by the collar.

"You're stretching it; you're stretching my shirt!" He cried out.

Sena let go and let out a sigh.

"It's important that you're able to see."

Rick sighed. She was right. He really couldn't see all too well while reading earlier.

"Fine." He muttered.

*

"Try these on." The glasses specialist instructed, forcing the glasses on Rick.

"Hm." He studied Rick and the glasses.

"What do you think?" The specialist asked.

"There aren't that many pairs with your prescription, but I think they suit you quite nicely."

Rick studied himself in the mirror. He never thought of red as his color. Yet he liked them nonetheless.

"I'll take them." He said, letting out a sigh as he smiled.

He then glanced around the shop to see what the girls were up to.

"I like these!" Maru smiled as she put on a pair of dark blue circular glasses.

"They fit you quite nicely!" Sena beamed.

Rick couldn't help but smile.

"Alright, Mr. Summers," the specialist began.

"Your payment is set; come see us if you ever need an adjustment."

Rick stepped out of his chair.

"Thank you." He said, waving goodbye to the specialist.

*

"What a day!" Sena giggled.

Rick nodded.

As they got to the door, he remembered earlier today about Abbey's visit.

"By the way, Sena." He began.

"Your friend came over to get some of her belongings."

Sena suddenly stopped.

"She's back?" Sena sounded surprised.

"Yeah, well,"

"Why didn't she text or call me?" She frowned, looking down at her phone.

"Well-"

"I'm sorry, Rick, Maru." She cut him off.

"I have to get home." She said turning around.

"I hope she's there." She quickly added as she ran off.

Maru turned to Rick, who was watching Sena drive off.

*

"Rick!" Maru began as she was busy hopping up and down.

"Yeah?" He turned to her.

"Oi, you'll get a headache if you don't stop."

Maru immediately stopped.

"We got you a present today!" She beamed.

"A present?" Rick repeated as he turned his attention back to his crossword puzzle.

"Look!" She said, puffing her cheeks.

"Huh?" He looked over and saw her holding up a shirt. It was yellow, with two bars at the bottom right, with yellow dots in them.

"Try it on!" She exclaimed, running over to him.

"Oi, Oi, easy there, bull girl." He laughed.

The last thing he needed was her to topple him with her inhuman strength. He noted earlier this week that her powers were now in full swing. She could easily pick him up. However, he was hesitant to inform her about her powers. She seemed blissfully unaware.

"Do you like it?" She asked with a hint of impatience.

"I guess it fits fine." He said, studying the color choice.

"We got yellow because Sena said you need to lighten up!" She beamed.

"Oh, really now?" Rick asked, giving an annoyed smile.

"Well, I like it." He sighed, smiling.

6 Rainbow

A few days passed since the sign on Sena's Flowers' door read 'closed.' Sena hadn't responded to Rick's texts either.

Rick put down the phone and sighed.

"Yeesh, what a disappointing day." He turned to Maru, who was staring out the window.

"Mm." She responded, not taking her glance off the window.

"What's wrong, kiddo?" Rick walked over to the couch and sat down next to her.

"I wanted to go to the park today." She pouted.

"Don't worry," Rick began.

"There'll be several other opportunities to go to the park, just not today."

He smiled, twirling her hair between his fingers.

"Mm..." Maru nodded, still pouting.

"Ah, wait," Rick began.

Maru turned her head towards him in confusion.

"I just remembered I need to get groceries." He clicked his tongue in annoyance.

"Do you want anything while I'm gone?" Rick questioned, turning his head to Maru.

"Hmm…" Maru bit her lip while in thought.

"Strawberries!" She beamed.

"Got it." Rick smiled, giving a wave as he walked out the door.

*

"Man, I really hate this kind of gloomy weather." He mumbled.

"Especially walking in it."

As he was walking, he turned his head to a building with a sign on it that read 'space available.'

The sign, however, wasn't what caught his attention. It was the woman sitting under it that did. Is that-

"Oi!" He shouted.

The woman didn't look up. She was sitting with her arms hugging her legs with her head down.

"Abbey!" He shouted once more.

She looked up, startled. She then put her head down once more.

"Go away." She muttered quietly.

Rick hustled over.

"You'll catch a cold," he began.

"So, what?" She said, not budging.

Rick scratched his head.

"Does Sena know you're out here getting drenched?"

She looked up.

"It's none of her concern."

"Do you know what used to be here?" He asked, eyeing the sign.

Abbey gave a hard look, then sighed.

"It was my father's dojo."

"Ah." Rick nodded.

"I couldn't do it." She whispered.

"Hm?" Rick leaned closer to hear better.

"I couldn't save him or his precious dojo!" She began to shake.

"When he got sick," she began; however, she quickly fell silent.

Rick cocked his head.

"I don't want to bore you with any tasteless detail-"

She stopped and watched as Rick sat next to her, holding the umbrella over her head.

"What?" Her eyes began to water.

"I want to know every tasteless detail if that's what it takes to get you and me out of this rain." He smiled.

A couple of tears streamed down her face as she gave a slight nod.

"My father was a man who loved kids."

Rick nodded.

"What he loved, even more, were swords." She paused.

"I wasn't born yet, but he tells me one day while polishing one of his favorite swords, he had an aha moment." She chuckled.

"Which was?" Rick questioned.

She closed her eyes and smiled.

"Why not combine the two?"

Rick smiled nodding.

"So, he opened this dojo." She motioned her hand towards the building.

"I was his only child, but he didn't mind at all." She closed her eyes.

"As long as I would learn to love the sword the same as him, he would be content."

She let out a sigh.

"And, of course, I did." She looked up.

"He taught me what he taught every one of his students."

"Which was?" Rick asked while cleaning his glasses.

"To love the sword." She smiled to herself.

"Oh, hey!" She exclaimed as she looked up.

"Look!" She said, pointing.

Rick put his glasses back on and looked.

It had finally stopped raining.

What was left from the bitter rain was now a beautiful rainbow.

Rick looked towards Abbey with a unique twinkle in her eyes. He smiled.

"It sure is beautiful." He smiled as he looked up.

7 Manhunt

"Thank you again, Rick." Abbey smiled as she stepped foot into her home.

"No need to thank me, just tell Sena I said hi." He smiled.

"Goodnight." She said, shutting the door.

*

"Hey, kiddo, I'm home!" Rick called up as he was walking up the steps. Maru rushed over to greet him at the door.

"What took you so long?" She huffed. Rick laughed, and then realized he hadn't gotten the groceries.

"Uh," Rick began as he scratched his head.

"I forgot." He chuckled. Maru looked at him, confused.

"You forgot?" She asked.

Rick sighed.

"It stopped raining; if you want to come, we can go now."

Maru's eyes twinkled. She grabbed his arm, not realizing her own strength as she pulled him down the steps.

"Wait!" Rick cried.

"You need a coat!"

*

"Ready now?" Rick asked, fixing her coat.

"Mm!" Maru smiled excitedly.

"Can we go to the park?" She questioned as they walked out the door.

"We can't go today; it's going to get dark soon."

Maru frowned.

"Plus," Rick added.

"Everything will be wet; you don't want that."

Maru nodded her head.

"Don't want that!" She repeated.

*

As they left the market, Rick had an uneasy feeling. He couldn't make sense of it either.

"Oi, Maru," he began.

"Hold my hand."

Maru looked up at him.

"Are you scared?"

Rick looked down.

"Huh!?" He cried, offended.

"Are you scared of the dark?" Maru repeated innocently.

"No, don't be silly!" Rick huffed.

As he was busy ranting about how people his age shouldn't fear something as silly as the dark, a group of men walked over.

Rick quickly looked up.

"Found you..." one of the men smirked.

A bunch of men suddenly surrounded the two. Cornered, Rick gripped Maru tightly. Maru looked pale as if the color in her face drained.

"Rick..." she whimpered.

"Oi." The men and Rick whipped their heads around.

"Do you have them?" A man questioned.

"Yes, Mr. Huser, sir."

The man grinned.

"Excellent, let's get this game of manhunt over with then, shall we?"

8 Chance Encounter

"Rick Summers," the man brushed by a few of the men.

"I've been dying to meet you." He grinned.

"I get that a lot." Rick chuckled nervously.

The man laughed.

"And he has a good sense of humor."

The man towered over Maru.

"I'm afraid you can't joke your way out of this one, however."

Rick grinned.

"Bet?"

The man laughed once more.

"You're quite amusing; it's a shame I was sent to do this."

Rick looked around cautiously as he tightened his grip on Maru.

"Hand her over." The man demanded.

Rick laughed. He just kept laughing.

The man looked shocked.

"Oi Oi, what's so funny about what I said?" He asked cautiously.

"It's just not my style to fight in front of a kid, you know?"

The man smirked.

"Well, who said you had to fight?" He asked.

"Just hand her over."

Rick knew he was at a disadvantage. The man could easily order his men to attack, and he was outnumbered.

"What would you gain from it?" Rick questioned.

The man frowned.

"What do you mean what would I gain from what?"

Rick sighed.

"What would you gain from taking her?" He asked.

The man was baffled by the question.

"Well, nothing. I'm afraid it's just orders."

Rick smiled smugly.

"Are you happy about working for such a job?"

The man opened his mouth to retort but shut it quickly.

"I got tired of seeing these people treated as lesser beings than us. It made me sick." Rick looked down at Maru.

"They deserve to live a hopeful life, just like us." He smiled as he patted her head.

"Rick..." Maru teared up.

The man scratched his head.

"Huser, sir," one of the men interrupted.

"Yo?" The man began again.

"What are we-"

The man then smiled.

"Retreat."

The men went into an uproar of shock.

"Boss, are you sure!?" One man cried.

"Let them pass now." The man demanded.

The men carefully stepped aside.

Rick stared in awe.

"What are you starin' for?" He asked.

"I said you could go." The man laughed.

"I hope you're not looking for a thank you or anything," Rick began as he picked up Maru.

"You interrupted our grocery run, and now they're probably closed."

Rick covered Maru's ears quickly.

"Bastard." He grinned.

The man then let out a hardy laugh.

"None taken." He said as he turned away.

"Come on, boys." He shouted.

Rick smiled.

Maru looked up at him.

"Rick?" She squeaked.

"Yeah, kiddo?" Rick quickly turned his attention to her.

"Are we going home now?" She asked.

Rick chuckled.

"Yep!" He smiled as he held her and walked.

*

"Mr. Huser?" A man questioned.

"What are you doing with your stuff?"

The man turned.

"Isn't it obvious?" He chuckled.

"I've had enough of this hell hole, time to get out of here."

He then turned to face the man.

"Also, Clark," he began.

"I've told you just call me Chris."

9 Atonement

About a week had passed since the incident; however, Maru had seemingly moved on from it.

While Maru quickly moved on, Rick had his concerns.

What if the man's call for the retreat was a hoax of some sort? What if he reported back, arranged something else, or had bigger plans?

He couldn't be sure.

"Rick?" There was a knock at the door.

"It's open, Sena," Rick answered.

The door opened to reveal Sena with a man behind her. Rick's eyes widened as his heart began to race.

It was the man who led the rest of the men during the attempted kidnapping.

"What are you-" Rick stammered.

"Is something wrong?" Sena asked, looking at him in confusion.

"Sena-" Rick began.

"Can I talk to you?"

Sena looked at the man and back to Rick.

"Of course."

Rick pulled her to the kitchen.

"What are you doing!?" He whispered angrily.

"What do you mean?" She frowned.

"Isn't he a friend of yours?"

Rick quickly turned his head towards the doorway.

The man was checking his watch.

"What made you think that!?" Rick sighed.

"You shouldn't trust people so easily, Sena."

Sena stared at him in confusion.

"So, he's not your friend?" Sena questioned.

"Look, let me handle this; you go downstairs." He turned his head once more.

"Don't let people you don't know in next time."

Sena nodded her head.

"I let you live here the day I met you, though." She smiled as she walked away.

Rick let out a sigh once more.

"Oi." He began.

"I don't know why my landlady let you in, but I'm not as nice as her, get out."

The man looked up.

"Sorry..." He smiled.

"However, I needed to talk to you."

Rick tapped his foot impatiently.

"Well, whatever it is, it doesn't matter to me."

Rick glanced towards his bedroom, where Maru was busy watching cartoons.

"Look," the man began.

"I think we got off on the wrong foot and-"

Rick laughed.

"Wrong foot?" He questioned.

"Try the fact that you tried kidnapping the kid in my care!"

The man sighed.

"About that,"

Rick had heard enough. He didn't want to shout in case Maru heard him, but he was nearing the end of his patience.

"Summers," the man continued.

"I quit my job the night of the incident."

Rick looked up quickly.

"I'm here because I wanted to thank you." The man smiled.

"It's just like you said," the man paused.

"When you asked if I was happy working such a job, it hit me." He looked down, smiling sadly.

"I never once was happy working at the Labs."

Rick looked down in silence. It seemed the man was sincere.

"What's your name?"

The man looked up at Rick.

"My name?" He smiled.

"It's Chris Huser."

Rick looked up, locking eyes with Chris.

"Damn." He smirked, looking back down steadily.

"I can tell you're sincere, and I hate it."

Chris looked down.

"Yep…" He said, twiddling his fingers.

"Where's my proper thank you?"

Chris looked up quickly.

"You said you had to thank me?"

Chris chuckled.

"You're really quite a character, Summers." He said in amusement.

"Well," the man began.

"Thank you for showing me what a miserable life I was leading."

He then paused.

"Thank you for not easily forgiving me; I know I have to atone for my sins."

Rick laughed.

Chris looked up, confused.

"Oi, what's so funny about what I said?" He asked in annoyance.

"Nothing," Rick kept laughing.

"I guess I owe Sena an apology; I'm just like her, forgiving so easily."

He smiled.

"Guess it can't be helped; I'm also just like you."

Chris cocked his head.

"What do you mean?" He questioned.

Rick looked at him.

"We both have sins we must atone for."

Chris smirked.

"Damn, didn't expect you to get so deep, Summers."

Rick chuckled.

"Cut the Summers bullshit, will you?" He glanced at the door again.

"I like my friends calling me Rick."

"Guess we'll be atoning together then," Chris said with a laugh.

10 Trust

After their unlikely friendship had begun, Chris frequently visited Rick's house, much to Rick's annoyance.

"Hey, what're you doing?" Chris asked while hovering over his shoulder.

Rick sighed while grabbing his pen.

"Looking for a new job, I guess."

Chris laughed.

"Hey, hey, don't laugh right in my ear, idiot."

Chris smiled, amused.

"I already have one kid I'm taking care of; I really don't need another," Rick smirked.

"Hey!" Chris shouted, insulted.

"By the way, where is the shrimp?" Chris questioned.

"The huh?" Rick scratched his head in annoyance.

"Maru," Chris replied.

"Oh, Sena and Abbey took her to the park." Rick checked the clock.

"I think they'll be back soon."

Chris nodded.

"Any luck finding anything?"

Rick grinned, annoyed.

"Not if you keep bothering me."

Chris looked at his watch.

"Ah shit, I have to go; tell them I said hi!" Chris said as he turned towards the door.

"By the way, I heard the school in this town is hiring." He said as he walked out.

Rick lifted his head.

"Huh?" But the door closed.

Rick sighed as he got up to fix himself a glass of water. He checked his phone to see what school was nearby.

"Elementary?" He clicked the link to the school's website.

*

"Science teacher?" Sena asked, cocking her head.

Rick smiled widely.

"You want to be a science teacher?" Sena repeated as she sat on the couch.

"Yeah, I mean not to brag or anything, but science was my best subject."

Sena looked at Abbey.

"What's the pay like?" Abbey asked as she leaned against the counter.

"It's ok, I guess, about as good as it gets," Rick answered.

"Do you think you could do it, you know, with Maru and all-"

Before Abbey could continue, Rick turned around with a sheepish grin on his face.

"Oi, I don't like that look, Summers," Abbey said, giving an annoyed smile.

"Well," Rick began.

"I was hoping two of my wonderful friends could maybe watch her during the day," Rick said as he quickly spun his chair away.

Sena and Abbey looked at each other.

"Rick," Sena began.

"We could certainly do it, but not if we have plans."

Rick spun himself toward them.

"I have Chris, too." He replied.

"You really trust that hyena-sounding numbskull?" Abbey huffed as she placed her hands on her hips.

"Hey-" Before he could continue, Maru chimed in.

"I can watch myself." She said sheepishly swinging her legs.

The three adults turned their attention toward her.

"No, you can't." They said in unison.

Maru puffed her cheeks in annoyance and folded her arms.

"Anyway, if there are days you guys, or Chris, can't do it, worst case, I'll just get a babysitter, I guess."

Sena and Abbey exchanged looks, then turned back toward Rick.

"Fine." They nodded their heads.

Rick smiled happily, humming as he continued to fill out his application.

11 Acceptance

"Rick?" A small voice called across the room.

"What's up, Maru?" Rick answered, not picking up his head.

The girl walked over to the kitchenette, where he was sitting reading the newspaper.

"I'm hungry," Maru whined.

Rick nodded his head, flipping a page of the paper. He then quickly looked up.

"You haven't eaten?" He questioned.

Maru nodded sadly.

Rick chuckled nervously.

"C'mon, we'll go grab something from the cafe."

Maru's eyes suddenly lit up.

"Can I get a cheesecake!?" She shouted excitedly.

Before Rick could answer, the girl ran to go put her shoes on.

Rick let out a sigh.

*

"I told you to hold my hand while we cross the street, Maru!" Rick scolded the girl.

Maru smiled sheepishly and gripped his hand.

Rick bit his lip as not to let out a noise of pain.

The girl could not, for the life of her, control her strength. Even when doing simple things such as holding someone's hand. Whether it be Rick, Sena, or whoever, it takes a lot for the victim of her touch not to wince in pain. And if the sound of pain slips, no one has the heart to tell the girl.

"We're here!" The girl pointed at the sign excitedly.

Rick sighed in relief as he cracked his wrist.

*

"Oh, good morning Rick, Maru!" The waitress smiled at the two.

"Morning, Bonnie." Rick gave a smile while removing Maru's hat as the girl waved.

"What can I do for you two this morning?"

Rick skimmed the menu for a second; as he opened his mouth to answer, Maru nudged him with her head.

"What's up, kiddo?"

"May I please get the cheesecake?" She whispered.

Rick chuckled.

"Yeah, sure." He said.

Maru beamed.

"Bonnie, could I get the French toast and a coffee, please?"

Bonnie nodded.

"Mm!"

Bonnie then turned to Maru.

Rick, knowing by now Maru, liked him to order for her, looked up sheepishly.

"She'll get a slice of cheesecake and a glass of chocolate milk, please."

Bonnie smiled.

"Ok, sounds great!" She smiled, walking away.

Rick then turned his attention toward Maru, who was busy coloring.

"Wow, kiddo, the professionals would be jealous of your coloring skills!"

Maru quickly looked up, blushing.

"Really!?" She questioned eagerly.

"Mm!" Rick smiled, patting her head.

*

"Here you go, enjoy!"

Bonnie said, smiling as she placed the food down.

"Thanks, Bonnie." Rick smiled.

Maru quickly lifted her fork and took a bite of her cheesecake eagerly.

Rick couldn't help but laugh.

"How is it, kiddo?" He asked as he picked up a napkin to wipe her face full of crumbs.

Maru nodded her head happily.

As Rick was about to take a bite of his breakfast, a man hesitantly came over.

"Excuse me?"

Rick put his fork down.

"Hi." Rick tried to hide the confusion in his voice.

"I'm with the school board of this town; you're not Rick Summers by chance, are you?"

Rick felt a flutter in his chest.

"Yeah, that's me!" He replied with a big smile.

"Ah, fantastic! Allow me to introduce myself properly; my name is Jeff Davis." The man extended his hand.

Rick quickly stood up to shake the man's hand.

 "A pleasure to meet you, sir." Rick smiled.

"Sorry to interrupt your breakfast with your daddy, sweetheart." The man smiled down at Maru.

Maru, who was too busy enjoying her breakfast, looked up, confused.

"Ah, anyway, we had problems with our phone systems for the past few days."

The man then looked Rick in the eyes.

"We'd like to invite you to be Wildwood Elementary school's new science teacher." He smiled.

Rick tried his best to suppress his glee.

 "I-I would love to." Rick quickly stammered.

"I mean, yes, that sounds great." He said, trying to catch himself.

The man let out a hardy laugh.

"Fantastic, we'd love to have you start next Monday then." The man smiled.

Rick beamed.

"Thank you, sir, sounds great!"

The men shook hands again. Jeff then walked away.

Maru swallowed her last piece of cheesecake as Rick sat back down. He ruffled her hair happily.

12 Lessons

"Hey, where are you going?" The girl tugged the man's coat.

Rick sighed as he knelt on his knee and faced the girl.

"I told you already, didn't I?" Rick smiled softly and began to gently stroke her hair.

Maru bit her lip as not to cry.

"Oi, why are you crying?" Rick looked concerned.

Maru puffed her cheeks.

"I'm not crying!" She pouted.

Rick chuckled.

"I promise I'll be back soon!" He stood up and gave the girl a quick head pat.

"Promise, promise?" The girl turned to him as he began descending the stairs.

"Promise, promise!" He shouted with a wave goodbye.

As she heard the door close, the girl let out a whimper.

This was the first time the two of them wouldn't be together since they met.

*

"Morning, shrimp!"

A tall man opened the door to the apartment. Maru turned her head to look at the man.

"Chris?" Maru asked as she stood up.

"What's with the concern in your voice, kiddo? He chuckled.

"Of course, it's me!" The man replied teasingly.

Maru let out a sigh as the man sat down at the kitchenette.

*

"Ah, here's your ID, Mr. Summers."

 The woman smiled, handing Rick his new school ID.

"Thanks a lot." He smiled as he began walking down the halls of Wildwood Elementary.

Classes were not in session yet; only a few teachers were at the school so far due to early morning meetings.

"Oh, you must be our new science teacher?"

Rick turned his head around quickly.

"Oh, sorry, didn't mean to startle you." A woman walked out towards the entryway of her classroom.

Rick turned to the woman.

"U-uh yeah, that's me!" He laughed nervously.

This woman was gorgeous! Rick couldn't help but stammer like a mess.

The woman extended her hand.

"Ms. Hoffman." She smiled. Rick extended his shaky hand.

"Summers, uh, sorry, I mean Rick Summers!" He smiled.

The woman examined him for a moment.

"You look awfully familiar..." She frowned.

Rick was too busy looking down.

"Uh, you can let go now, by the way." She smiled.

"O-oh, right!" Rick quickly put his hand to his side.

"What do you teach?" He questioned.

"English." Ms. Hoffman smiled.

"Ah, cool!" He looked around the hallway.

"You-"Before he could finish, a bell began to ring.

"That's the bell for the kid's busses; I'm afraid I have to go get prepared for today." Ms. Hoffman laughed.

"See you later, Rick." She smiled as she closed the door.

"A-Ah, see you!" Rick blushed as he turned away.

Damnit, Summers, pull yourself together! He thought as he was walking down the hallway to his classroom.

He then paused. Is somebody there...? Rick turned to a beam where a girl poked her head out but quickly hid again.

Rick walked around the beam to see who it was. The girl was too old to be an elementary student but too young to be a teacher.

"Yo." Rick placed his hand on the beam, cornering the girl.

"E-eh!?" The girl blushed a deep red.

"I-it's not what you think!" She stammered wildly.

"You know, kids will be coming in soon; what will they think if they see you hiding and gawking at a teacher?" He then let out a sigh.

The girl looked down quickly.

"It's just," the girl began.

"I-I'm not good at introducing myself, especially not to c- g-guys!" She stammered wildly.

Rick took his hand off the beam and sighed.

"P-plus, weren't you just blushing...?"

The girl quickly went pale, realizing what she had just said.

Rick turned red.

"H-huh!?" He turned to her quickly.

"H-how'd you-"

The girl bowed her head.

"I'm so sorry!" She kept her head bowed in what seemed like a shame.

"My name is Tammy, and I'll be your assistant for this week!" She slowly raised her head and gave a nervous smile.

Rick scratched his head and sighed.

"Alright, Tammy." He smiled.

"Let's not pull this crap in the classroom, ok?"

Tammy nodded her head hard.

"Oi, you'll get a headache!" He put his hand on her shoulder.

Tammy suddenly stopped.

"T-this way!" Tammy pointed to the classroom door.

"That's where w- y-you'll be teaching!" She smiled.

Rick let out a sigh and smiled.

"Let's get going then." He said as they began walking towards the room.

13 Pinky Promise

The weekend had come after a busy beginning at Wildwood Elementary.

Maru and Rick were seated on the couch, watching cartoons as they heard a sudden knock at the door.

"Rick?"

Rick looked up, half asleep.

"Chris?" He sleepily replied.

The door flung open.

"Oi! Why are you trying to break my door down?" Rick cried angrily.

"Rick," Chris began.

"That certainly is my name." Rick let out a sigh.

"You're not going to believe this."

Rick sat up.

"What am I not going to believe?" He asked.

Chris brushed his hair back.

"Experiment Labs,"

Rick's eyes widened.

"Well," Chris continued.

"There was a rebellion by a few of the patients, they kidnapped the boss's son, and now the labs are in ruins."

Rick quickly turned to Maru, whose eyes were filled with fear.

"Chris," Rick began.

"Are there any survivors?"

Chris let out a sigh.

"I volunteered to go back tonight with a few of my guys, but I highly doubt it."

Maru looked down at the floor.

"247..." She whispered.

"Maru," Rick began.

Her eyes began to fill with tears.

"Why?" She whimpered.

Chris scratched his head.

"I don't know, kiddo. I just don't know."

Maru turned to Rick with pleading eyes.

Rick stared momentarily. *What does she want? Does she want a hug...?*

Before he could say anything, the girl clung to him, wildly sobbing into his chest. The two men exchanged nervous looks. He then began gently stroking her head.

"Maru..." he whispered.

"It'll be ok." He reassured her.

"I promise." He said.

Maru looked up at him.

"You really promise?" She asked, sniffling.

Crap. He knew he shouldn't have used such a heavy word such as 'promise,' but if it was what she needed to hear.

"Mm, I promise."

His heart sunk. Thinking about how he'd already made a promise, he knew he couldn't go back on.

Rick cupped the girl's tiny face in his hands.

"I promise you, Maru, everything will be ok; I'm here for you no matter what, 'kay?"

Maru's eyes widened.

"Oof."

Rick quickly shot Chris a dirty look.

"Now, why don't you go inside and relax?" Maru nodded.

"Wait," she said, standing up.

"Mm?"

She smiled.

"Pinky promise?" Rick looked up quickly and smiled.

"Ah," he said, raising his pinky.

"I pinky promise that no matter what, I'll protect you." He smiled as they swore on it.

14 Beneath the Rubble

"Chris, sir?" A man knocked on the door.

"Clark?"

"Yes, sir."

"C'mon in." The man opened the door.

"Sir," Chris shot him a dirty look.

"...Chris," the man corrected himself.

"Get on with it, Clark." Chris raised an eyebrow.

"W-well Chris," Clark stammered. "Before we came the other night to investigate the Labs, we set up cameras." Chris sat up a bit.

"And?"

Clark handed him a camera.

"Well, this...this isn't one of our men." As Chris pressed play, his eyes widened.

"Is that..."

*

A man wandered the rubble whistling, swinging his keys.

"Yeesh." He sighed as he kicked a tiny piece of the ruin.

"Glad I wasn't on shift during this shitstorm."

The man suddenly froze. He looked around cautiously. *There's no way.*

Before the man could take another step, something grabbed at his leg. Startled, the man dropped his keys.

"Huh!?" He looked down quickly.

"I said...help." The girl looked up at him.

Her grip was weak, and yet he couldn't free himself. All he could do was stare.

"Please..." The girl weakly mumbled.

"H-hold on..." the man said.

"Let go a sec."

The girl opened her mouth but shut it.

"I'm not going to run; just let go."

She gave what seemed to be an attempt at a nod. The man knelt and smirked.

"I knew stealing this thing would have its benefits." He said, dipping his finger in a tiny bottle labeled 'The Cure.' He then proceeded to apply it to the girl's lips.

"Don't get mad at me if this doesn't work, kid."

The girl's eyes widened.

"Huh," the man said, closing the bottle.

"Guess it did work." The girl stared at the man in awe.

"Mister." She began.

"What's your name?"

The man smiled as he began picking pieces of the rubble off the girl.

"Norio Takeshi..."

*

Chris stared as the recording ended in astonishment.

"You know him, S-...Chris?"

Chris shook his head.

"Barely," he said.

"He didn't seem like the type of guy to play the hero." He said, handing the camera back to Clark.

"Do you think that's what he went there to do?"

Chris scratched his head.

"Beats me; quit asking so many questions." He scolded.

"I'm only teasing you," Chris said, chuckling.

Clark let out a sigh of relief.

"Understood!" He said, giving a nervous laugh.

*

"...Norio?" The girl asked as the man lifted her onto his back.

"Mm." He replied.

"...Like the cookie?" She asked.

Norio quickly stopped.

"Oi!" He cried.

"Don't compare my name to a cookie, you brat!" He shouted angrily.

The girl let out a laugh.

Norio sighed as he continued walking.

"Mother's going to kill me for this…" He muttered as he carried 247 back home.

15 Bandaged

"A child...?" A woman questioned.

"Clearly." The man huffed in response.

"Yeesh, what are you in such a mood for, big brother?" Another girl chimed in.

"Tea is ready." A third girl said as she walked into the room.

The three girls and Norio sat around a table in silence.

"What do you think mother will think, Nori?" The eldest girl began.

"What does mother care?" Norio sighed.

"It's not like she's ever around anyway." He went to take a sip of his tea.

"Big bro has a good point." The youngest of the three girls said.

"Yui, let us handle this, please."

Yui puffed her cheeks in annoyance.

"Faye?"

The eldest turned to the middle child.

"Eh?" Faye looked back.

"Hiromi," she began.

"I personally think mother would be delighted, you know since-" Faye quickly turned to look at Norio and Yui.

"She loves them as if they were her own."

Hiromi let out a sigh.

"You know mother won't be home for another few weeks, Nori, right?"

Norio looked up.

"Mm."

*

Norio walked next door to his house after the chat with his sisters, 247 on the couch.

"Oh." He said, walking in.

"You're still awake."

247 looked up.

"I can't sleep."

Norio walked over.

"How come?"

The girl looked down.

"This couch is too uncomfortable."

Eh? That's the only reason!? Norio sighed.

"Well, you'll just have to deal with it."

The girl looked up.

"Where am I going?"

Norio raised his eyebrow.

"What do you mean?" He questioned.

"Do you really want a monster here with you?" The girl looked down quickly.

"Hah?" He looked around.

"What the heck do you mean?"

The girl let out tears of frustration.

"I'm not human anymore, you know."

Norio studied her.

"I don't see any non-human qualities from you."

The girl looked up quickly.

"You don't get it, do you!?" She cried out.

"That place made me a freak!" She sobbed as she pointed to her right arm.

Norio bent down and lifted her arm.

The girl's arm twitched.

"What did they inject you with?" He questioned, holding her arm.

The girl looked down.

"Did you hear me?"

The girl sniffled.

"I don't know, but my arm hurts sometimes, and it gets all...weird." She replied, still looking down.

"Mm." He said, laying her arm gently on her lap.

"One sec." He said as he got up.

"Tch, my back." He grunted as he stretched and walked to the bathroom.

The girl puffed her cheeks but was surprised as he quickly came back out.

"What is that...?" She asked, pointing at what he was holding in his hand.

He pointed to the right side of his face.

"These things, bandages." He knelt and took her left arm into his hand.

"What are you-"

Norio began wrapping her arm in bandages.

"Not certain if that'll work or not, but maybe your arm might stop twitching." He said as he finished wrapping.

The girl looked up tearfully.

"Nori-"

Norio let out a loud yawn.

"Listen, it's been a long day; I'm going to bed." He said, shutting the lights in the living room while walking into his room.

"B-"The girl turned.

"Enjoy my comfy couch, kid." He waved, shutting the door to his room.

The girl stared at the shut door for a few moments before looking down at her bandaged arm.

"Thank you..." she smiled softly.

Suddenly, the door opened.

"I don't need it on my conscience that you froze to death." He said, quickly chucking blankets at her.

"Night." He said, shutting his door again.

The girl huffed as she pulled the blanket onto herself.

"Goodnight." She whispered as she quickly drifted off to sleep.

*

A few moments later, the door creaked open; Norio smiled as he looked at the tiny girl fast asleep.

As he quietly shut the door, he walked over to a picture of two boys and a girl.

He let out a sigh. And got into his bed.

"I wonder what he would do..." He said, staring up at the ceiling.

Rick, wherever you are... He thought as he drifted off to sleep.

16 Warmth

Norio shut the newspaper and huffed.

"Looks like I'm officially out of a job."

He sighed as he sank back into the couch.

"I'm surprised." She began.

"I didn't think you would be upset about it," Faye said as she placed tea down on the table.

"You've said several times that you didn't enjoy work at such a place."

Norio picked up the tea and blew on it a couple of times before taking a sip.

"Weren't you working there because you had heard rumors your bro-"

Norio turned with a glare.

Faye let out a sigh.

"What's got you in such a bad mood this morning, baby brother?" Hiromi questioned as she sat on the arm of the couch, playing with his hair.

"I didn't sleep well, I guess." He muttered.

"Oh!" Faye exclaimed as if she had just remembered something.

"What's up with you?" Norio turned to her.

"It felt like a dream," she giggled.

"I mean, since it happened so suddenly, but where is that little girl?"

Norio sat up a bit, resting his face on his hand.

"She's still asleep."

Faye turned to Hiromi.

"Poor thing, she must be exhausted."

Hiromi smiled.

"That one over there, on the other hand, has no reason to be."

The three turned to look at Yui, who was sound asleep with her mouth wide open.

"She really should fix her sleep schedule before mother comes back," Hiromi said as she let out a sigh.

"Speaking of that girl," Faye began.

"What's her name?"

Norio quickly looked up.

"Well-" He began but was cut off with a knock at the door. Norio got up.

"Wait, Nori!" Faye exclaimed.

"Hah?" He turned to face her as the door opened.

"Never mind..." she grumbled.

Standing outside the door was 247.

"Oh, morning," Norio said, greeting her.

The girl walked past him.

Eh?

"Oh, my goodness!" Faye exclaimed.

"Nori, she's adorable!" She cried.

Before 247 could say anything, Faye began squishing her cheeks.

"Faye!" Hiromi shouted, slapping her hands away.

247 winced as she rubbed her cheeks.

"Cat got your tongue or what?"

The three quickly turned their attention toward Norio.

"No..." 247 walked over to him.

"How does your arm feel?" He asked.

"Why, what's wrong with her arm?" Hiromi asked with concern.

"Well-" Norio began, but 247 quickly cut him off.

"N-nothing!" She exclaimed.

Norio looked down at the girl and let out a sigh.

"Nori," the girl tugged at his shirt.

Norio bent down.

"I'm hungry..." The girl whispered.

Norio stood back up.

"Sorry, I'll come back later." He motioned at 247.

Hiromi and Faye looked at each other confused.

"Don't worry, everything's fine; she's just hungry." He said, opening the door.

247 quickly blushed.

"Oi! I whispered for a reason!" She grumbled as she followed him outside.

"I'll see you," Norio said as he shut the door.

The two girls stood there for a moment, extremely confused.

"Hah?" Yui slowly rose from her slumber, rubbing her eyes.

*

"What do you like?" Norio asked the girl, who was seated on the couch.

"I don't know." She answered as she swung her feet.

"Hah?" He turned to her.

"What the heck do you mean you don't know?"

The girl frowned.

"I mean, I haven't eaten anything but slop for a while!" She folded her arms and huffed in annoyance.

Norio ran his fingers through his hair and let out a frustrated sigh. He pulled out a recipe book. He sighed as he opened it.

"Pancakes, waffles, French toast, a better attitude, eggs, anything sounding good to you yet?"

The girl turned.

"Pancakes." She responded, puffing her cheeks.

"Dang, was kind of hoping you would go with a better attitude for sure." He smirked to himself.

"You're the one who needs a nicer attitude, you meanie!" She cried out.

"Here you go, princess."

Norio said, placing the plate in front of her.

247 stared down at the pancakes in silence for a few moments.

Norio walked back over.

"You don't get to be picky!" He cried.

"No." She said, steadily, looking down.

"Hah!?" He said as he gritted his teeth in annoyance.

"It's just," she smiled as tears began streaming down her face.

"I haven't had such a warm meal made for me in so long..."

17 Teachings

A few weeks had passed since Rick had begun teaching at Wildwood Elementary. Rick has always had a soft side for kids; teaching a subject in his field of knowledge was also a nice bonus.

As night began to fall, Rick was busy grading his class tests.

"Hey, Rick?" A small voice called out.

"Mm?" Rick answered, not picking his head up.

"What are you doing?" Maru came over, attempting to get a glimpse.

"Nothing," Rick replied, too, into the grading.

Maru puffed her cheeks.

"Liar!"

Rick turned his head, quickly coming out of the trance.

"Huh?"

Maru glared, still puffing her cheeks.

"Oi oi, take it easy." He chuckled, patting her head.

Maru finally gave up on puffing her cheeks and took a deep breath.

"What do you need?" Rick asked, twirling her hair.

Maru pointed.

"What does that say?" She asked.

Great. Now I totally lost my focus. Rick turned towards the test he was grading.

"What?"

Maru placed her finger on a word.

"This."

Rick looked.

"Ah, it says photosynthesis."

Maru stared at him, blankly for a few moments.

"...Say, Maru?" Rick said, breaking the silence.

Maru kept her head down.

"No, no! Hey! That's a difficult word, but..." He continued cautiously.

"Do you...have you learned how to read?"

Maru slowly lifted her head as she looked up.

"No..." She whispered.

"That's ok!" Rick smiled.

"You're only five, kiddo!"

Maru looked up quickly.

"Really!?" Rick chuckled nervously.

"Do you mean that at the fact that you're five years old, or-"

Maru huffed.

"I know I'm five!" She held out a hand, holding up all five of her fingers.

"See!" She cried.

Rick let out a hardy laugh.

"Kids don't usually learn how to read until they're six, or even seven." He said.

Maru's eyes lit up.

"Really!?" She exclaimed.

"Totally!" Rick laughed.

Maru climbed onto his lap and cupped his face in her tiny hands.

"Rick?" She stared into his eyes.

"Y-Yeah, what's up, kiddo?" Rick chuckled nervously.

Her grip was hurting him a bit.

"Teach me how to read?" She asked, giving that puppy-eyed look that kids tend to do when they want something.

"Oh, sure!" He smiled.

"I'd be more than happy to."

Maru let go as she hopped down.

"Yay!" She clapped her hands together, smiling widely.

Rick couldn't help but smile, too. *Damnit, this kid is way too adorable.* He thought.

"Now," Rick began, turning his chair back to his desk.

"Why don't you go to bed, so I can finish grading my kid's papers?"

Maru beamed.

"Aye aye, sir!" She said, turning away but quickly turned back.

Rick, now with his attention back on grading, quickly turned again.

"Hm?"

Maru kissed him on his cheek.

"I love you, Rick!" She giggled happily.

Rick turned a bright red.

"G-goodnight, Maru." He stammered, stroking her head gently.

*

As Rick got into bed, he stared at the ceiling.

"When was the last time I heard those words...?" He muttered as he turned onto his side.

Suddenly, a vivid memory of a smiling young boy flashed in his head.

"Ah...that's when." Rick sighed as he hugged his pillow.

18 Emersyn

Just as Norio was about to sit on the couch, he heard a knock at his door.

He let out a groan as he walked over to the door.

"Who's there?" He questioned.

"It's your sister."

Norio scratched his head.

"I have three; which one?"

Hiromi opened the door.

"Do you really not know our voices by now!?" She huffed as she entered.

"Come on in, I guess." He sighed.

"What are you freaking out for?" He asked, taking a seat.

"You know mother is coming home today, right?"

Norio slapped his hand to his head.

"Crap." He sighed.

"Nori, what are you going to tell her?" Hiromi looked at him.

"Hah?"

Hiromi pointed over to the room where 247 was napping.

"Oh, right."

Hiromi huffed.

"You can't just be so nonchalant about everything all of the time, you know!" She cried.

"Ah, is that so?" Norio said, staring blankly across the room.

"Seriously! You c-"

Before she could finish, the doorbell rang.

"Already!?" Hiromi cried out.

"Wake her up, quick!"

Norio sat up quickly.

"Yeah, great heads up, big sis."

Hiromi puffed her cheeks.

"At least I warned you at all, you little brat!"

Norio walked to the other room to wake the sleeping child.

Hiromi walked over to answer the door.

"Oi, wake up," Norio said, shaking the girl.

247 let out a sleepy whine.

"You can sleep later, 'kay?"

The girl slowly sat up, rubbing her eyes.

*

As he walked out of the room, Hiromi was greeted by an order to hang up their mother's coat.

Norio turned his head to see his mother, sitting sipping coffee.

"Mother-" He began.

"Where is she?"

Norio pointed toward the closet.

"She's hanging your coat-"

She narrowed her eyes.

"The child, Norio."

Norio scratched his head.

"Hey...kid?"

Crap! She doesn't have a name yet! He looked around frantically.

"Well?" His mother asked, keeping a cold gaze set on him.

"Yeah...she's right here." He pointed to 247, who just walked out of the room.

"Eh?" The girl stared, surprised at the new company.

Suddenly, her cold gaze softened as she saw the girl.

"Ho? And what is your name?"

The girl stared blankly, then up at Norio. She quickly tugged on his sleeve as he bent down.

"Hey, she wants my name!" She whispered frantically.

The lady stood up and started walking over.

"I'll start; my name is Masa." She smiled, extending her hand out to 247.

Norio smiled nervously, quickly shoving the girl over to his mother.

"Shake her hand!" He quickly mouthed.

247 shakily lifted her hand. Masa smiled as they shook hands.

As Hiromi walked out, she and Norio exchanged nervous looks.

"So, I heard you were fired," Masa said, turning to Norio.

He sighed.

"I didn't get fired or anything; everyone in my department lost their jobs due to the incident."

Masa frowned.

"I see." She turned to 247, who was seated on Norio's lap.

"That's where you met my son, is it not?"

Oi, mother! She's only five! You can't just ask her these kinds of questions! Norio thought.

Norio looked to Hiromi, who, in turn, shrugged.

"Mm." 247 replied.

"I see." Masa smiled.

"I guess they didn't bother giving you a name there, hm?"

Mother!? Norio looked up at 247, who was silent.

"They didn't." She looked down.

"How awful," Masa said sadly.

"Well, if you are to live here, you must be given a name."

247 looked up quickly. Norio and Hiromi turned quickly.

"Now, why does this seem like a surprise to you all?" She smiled.

"What, did you think I was going to turn this adorable yet rugged little girl away?"

She turned to Norio.

"I took you in, didn't I?"

Norio blushed.

"Yeah, I guess."

Masa stood up.

"Seeing my son helping someone in the same position he was once in, it's quite amazing." She chuckled.

Norio stared down at the floor.

Hiromi smiled.

"Well then," Masa began as she placed down her coffee mug.

"I'm exhausted and must take a nap; by the time it's dinner, I hope you can find this poor girl a name."

Norio quickly looked up.

"I was fortunate; you already came with one." She winked.

"Hiromi, my coat please, honey?"

Masa asked, standing up.

"Yes, mother." She walked over, ruffling 247 and Norio's heads, then grabbed the coat.

"I'll see you two in a few hours then." Masa smiled as she waved.

"Don't be late!" Hiromi waved, closing the door.

*

"Are you sure?" The girl questioned, sitting on the chair next to the man.

"Sure, about what?" He asked, not looking up from the computer.

"Can I really, really live here?"

Norio let out a sigh.

"What the hell do you think you've been doing?"

247 puffed her cheeks.

"But-"

Norio suddenly sat up in his seat.

"What?" She questioned.

"Nothing, just mind your own business, Emersyn."

The girl growled but quickly stopped.

"Eh?" She stood up, running over to his chair.

He smiled.

"I think this name suits you perfectly."

The girl skimmed the definition on the screen. Her eyes twinkled.

"Really!?" She quickly spun his chair around to face her.

"Really!?" She repeated.

"You better like it; I'm not changing it." He said, turning back towards the computer.

"No! I love it!" She cried.

Norio smiled softly as he went to bookmark the page.

"Emersyn." She beamed.

"Mm, Emersyn." He repeated, ruffling her hair.

19 Nightmare

"Emersyn?" Masa asked while washing the dishes.

"Yup," Norio replied.

"I see," she turned to the girl.

"I think it's a lovely name." She smiled.

"Anyway, do you mind if I go grab a drink?"

Masa turned around.

"Well...as long as you're responsible, what will you do with Emersyn?"

He turned to Emersyn, who was napping once again.

"She'll be fine; you don't mind?"

Masa nodded.

"I trust you greatly." She said, stroking his cheek.

"Thank you, Mother." He turned toward the door to leave.

"Nori...?"

Norio quickly turned.

"Where are you going?" Emersyn questioned as she sat up, wiping her eye.

"Uh, I'll be back later."

Emersyn held out her arms.

Eh?

"Carry me?" She looked up.

"F-fine..." Norio grumbled.

*

After tucking her in, Emersyn quickly fell asleep once more.

Norio sighed.

"Yeesh, what a handful you are." He said with a smile.

*

As Norio stepped into the bar, he took his coat off, hanging it on a coat rack.

He plopped down at the bar counter.

"What can I get for you?" A bartender asked.

As Norio opened his mouth to reply, the girl next started mumbling.

He quickly turned his attention back to the bartender.

"I'll take a shot of vodka, please."

The bartender nodded.

As he waited, he noticed the girl next to him, holding her head.

"Oi."

The girl didn't budge.

"You look like you're in pain."

He then heard the girl sniffle.

"Wow, nice observation, smarty pants."

Norio narrowed his eye.

"I sure as hell am in pain!" She began tugging his sleeve.

"If you're going to butt into a stranger's business, don't suddenly go ignoring them!"

Norio turned around with a glare.

"Don't tug my sleeve."

The girl puffed her cheeks.

"Don't be a dummy!" She cried.

Norio turned away again and let out a long sigh.

"I can't stand drunks."

The girl crossed her arms.

"The hell are you at a bar for then!?"

She cried.

"To de-stress!" He cried, getting up.

"Sorry, I've got a lot on my plate; hope whatever you're going through gets better for you soon." He said, walking across the room to a different seat.

The girl began laughing. As she was hysterical, her phone rang.

She quickly froze.

Suddenly, the bar doors slammed open.

"Found you, God damnit, Keren!" A man cried out.

The girl stumbled, trying to get up.

Norio, in the middle of a conversation with a bartender, quickly turned his attention toward the sudden noise.

"Ah crap, now what is she doing-"

His eye widened as he watched the girl get pushed to the floor.

Before he knew it, he was standing behind the man who had thrown her to the floor. Norio tapped his shoulder.

"Huh!?" The man turned around and met with Norio's fist.

The man quickly fell to the floor with a nosebleed.

Norio stood over him, fist-shaking.

"Listen up, you sack of shit," he began.

"She seems like a real pain in the ass but touch her again, and I'll-"

The man threw a punch, hitting Norio in the stomach.

"Stop it, both of you!" Keren cried out.

"I'm not going to fight!" Norio shouted, quickly dodging a punch.

"Who even are you, and why the fuck are you defending that bitch!?"

Keren began sobbing.

"I came here tonight for a drink in peace." He began as he pinned down the man's arms.

"Your friend, or whatever, began pestering me."

The man growled.

"I knew it! You cheating bitch!" He screamed.

"Not like that," Norio grumbled, struggling to keep him pinned down.

"She was upset; I can see why, dating piece 'a shit like you would send me bawling, too."

The man tried reaching up at Norio's face, Norio quickly slammed his arm back down.

"You bastard!" The man cried.

Keren stepped over.

"The cops are on their way."

The man's eyes went wild.

"You what!?" He shrieked.

Suddenly, cops filled the bar, grabbing the man.

"You'll pay for this; I'll find you!" The man cried out as they walked him out in cuffs.

Keren turned to Norio.

"Mister-" Norio turned away.

"You made a mess of my evening, is nothing easy?"
He sighed, leaning on the counter.

Keren whimpered.

 "I'm s-"

Norio glared.

"Don't apologize." He huffed.

"I don't know the whole deal, and you're probably too
drunk off your ass to give me the juicy details."

He looked up.

"Where do you live?"

Keren looked down.

"On the streets."

Norio huffed.

"Yeesh, I know you're drunk, but which str-"

Keren, still steadily looking down, frowned.

"You didn't hear me; I really mean the streets; I'm
fucked."

Norio looked at her in silence. He sighed, running his
fingers through his hair.

"Fine, tonight, I'll let you in at my place."

Keren quickly looked up.

"I have a kid at home, so you better keep your mouth shut."

Before Keren could answer, Norio held out his hand.

"I won't let him or anyone else hurt you."

Keren stared down, tearily eyed.

"On one condition." He said.

Keren quickly looked up.

"To me, alcohol is a treat, but only once in a while," he began.

"I don't know how you like to drink, but as I mentioned, I have a kid so I got rid of all my alcohol."

Keren nodded slowly.

"All I ask is if you agree to all of this, don't bring alcohol into my house." He sighed.

Keren looked up.

"You're too nice for your own good."

Norio turned away.

"Yeah, I guess I am." He muttered.

Keren laughed.

"By the way, I'm Norio." He held out his hand.

Keren momentarily studied his hand before grabbing it.

"Keren." She smiled.

"Are you sure about this, Norio?"

Norio shrugged.

"Got nothing to lose."

As they shook hands, Norio yawned.

"Let's go; I'm fricking exhausted." He said.

Keren stood up.

"Me too." She laughed.

*

As they got in the car, Keren laid her head against the window of the car.

Did I finally wake up from that nightmare...? She wondered as she drifted off into sleep.

20 Roomies

As morning came, Keren found herself awake in a strange environment.

She pulled the blanket off her head quickly.

"Not again..." She let out a sigh.

Then she quickly remembered the man from last night.

"Wait a minute..." Before she could finish, she heard a man and a girl talking.

She quickly pulled the blanket back over herself.

"What's that?" Emersyn asked, pointing at a lump on the couch.

"A person." Norio nonchalantly replied.

"Eh!?" Emersyn turned to him.

"Is it dead!?" She cried out, swinging at his stomach.

Norio bent down, placing a hand on her shoulder.

"Relax. Relax!" He cried.

Emersyn stopped and sniffled.

"Listen," he began.

"She'll be staying with us too, but temporarily."

Emersyn looked up teary-eyed.

"I think." He quickly added.

C'mon, Keren, make a good entrance, Keren thought to herself.

Suddenly, the blanket came flying off.

Norio and Emersyn quickly turned.

"That's right, kiddo! It looks like we're roomies n-" Before she could finish, her head began throbbing.

"Ow!" She let out a whimper.

"It hurts!"

"Here's your medicine. Next time, don't stand up too fast, idiot," Norio said, placing medication in front of her.

"Thanks..." Keren mumbled, holding an ice pack on her forehead.

"Anyways...!" Keren began.

"What's your name, kid?" She asked.

Emersyn, sitting on the opposite side of the table, looked up.

"It's Emersyn!" She beamed.

Norio leaning back on the wall, gave a tiny self-satisfied smile.

"Nori," Keren began.

"Hah?"

Keren looked at him for a moment.

"It's just; you look a bit...young."

Norio quickly turned.

"N- It's not like that! I'm not her dad!" He cried.

"Plus, I'm not that young; I'm 22!"

Keren stared.

"Hah!?" She cried. "What the hell do you mean, you're not her father!?"

While the two were busy bickering, Emersyn was busily involved with her drawing.

"Done!" She exclaimed, holding up her art.

"Hah!?" The two shouted in unison, turning to face her.

"Look!" She beamed.

"Is that a...cat?" Keren asked, studying the drawing.

Norio gave her a hard nudge.

"Don't question her; if you get it wrong, you'll hurt her feelings!" He whispered angrily.

"Yeah!" She giggled.

Keren looked at Norio and gave a prideful smirk.

*

As the day progressed, everyone in the house seemed to be getting increasingly bored.

"There's nothing to do!" Emersyn said, laying her head on Norio's lap.

"Can't be helped, quit whining." Norio scolded.

"Well," Keren began.

The two looked up.

"I was going to see the circus that's in town with my ex..." she smirked.

"But now that the loser's rotting in jail..."

Emersyn quickly sprang up.

"A circus!?" She cried.

Keren nodded.

"Got two tickets, and kids go for free!" She then turned to Norio.

"Eh, Norio?" She winked.

"When is it?" Norio asked, sounding like he could care less.

"It starts in..." She quickly checked her phone.

"Two days!"

Norio let out a sigh.

"Fine."

The two girls cheered happily.

21 Natural

As Rick stepped into the classroom, he let out a yawn.

"Oh, good morning, Rick!" Tammy waved.

"Hey." Rick smiled as he waved.

Due to their meeting, Rick was a bit weary working with Tammy. However, she seemed more than capable and proved to love the kids and her job overall.

"The buses should be coming soon!"

Rick nodded, sitting at his desk.

"Tammy," Rick began.

Tammy looked up from her phone, cocking her head.

"Did you do something different with your hair?"

Tammy blushed.

"Uh, no..." she laughed nervously.

"I just didn't have time to straighten it this morning."

Rick nodded.

"It's usually really wavy; I hate it." She smiled, looking down.

"Why?" Rick questioned.

"Huh, why what?" Tammy asked as she looked up.

"Why do you hate your natural hair?"

Tammy began twirling her hair.

"Well, I guess because I was teased a lot for it being messy."

Rick stood up.

"Is it hard to straighten it every morning?"

Tammy looked down.

"Y-yeah..."

Rick walked over and sat on top of a desk.

"I like it." He smiled, placing a hand on Tammy's shoulder.

Tammy looked up with tears in her eyes.

"R-really...?" She smiled, trying to hold back her tears."

Rick nodded.

"I think natural wavy suits you really nicely!" He said, flashing a big smile.

"R-Rick..." Tammy sniffled.

"Ah Crap," Rick said, quickly lifting his head.

"Eh?" Tammy looked confused, then the bells rang.

"Oh!" Tammy nodded, wiping her eyes quickly.

"Good talk!" She laughed.

Rick turned around.

"Mm, good talk." He smiled as he walked back to his desk.

*

"Good morning, Rick!" Tammy greeted as she stepped into the room.

"Good morning, Ta-" Rick quickly lifted his head from looking at papers.

"Oh!" He cried.

Tammy had cut her hair from back length to neck length, with a wave.

Tammy twirled.

"Do you like it?" She beamed.

"Who cares what I think? Do you like it?"

Tammy turned around.

"Mm! It's much more manageable this short, and I think the wave is a nice touch!" She giggled.

Rick gave a nod and smiled.

Then came a knock at the door.

"Mr. Summers," a voice called out.

"Ms. Hoffman!" Rick cried out.

"Oh, good morning, Annette!" Tammy waved.

"I have your copies, h-" She paused.

"Oh, your hair!" She pointed.

"Tammy, I love it!" She cried.

"Thank you so much!" Tammy laughed.

"I wouldn't have recognized you if it weren't for your voice!" Ms. Hoffman laughed.

"Anyways, I have to go back to class." She said as she gently plopped the papers down on Rick's desk.

Rick looked up.

"Thanks!" He nodded.

"You got it." She winked.

Rick nearly fell out of his chair.

"See you later, Tammy, Mr. Summers." She said, waving.

Tammy walked to the back of the room, humming.

"She's so pretty..." Rick whispered.

22 Fortunate

"Where are you going?" Emersyn asked as Norio put his coat on.

"Out." He replied.

Keren frowned.

"Yeah, no shit, where are you going?"

Norio sighed.

"To town, I need some peace."

Keren and Emersyn exchanged looks.

"You know, since two brat's kind of ruined that for me." He smirked.

"Later." He said, turning to the door.

"Oi! don't associate me with the word 'brat,' I'm only two years younger than you!" Keren cried.

"Yeah! I'm five!"

Keren turned to Emersyn quickly.

"Sorry, kid, you still qualify for the brat discount."

Emersyn turned.

"Eh!? Really!?" She cried.

By the time the two turned around, Norio was gone.

"What a jerk!" Keren cried, puffing her cheeks.

*

As Norio began roaming through town, he noticed a tent propped up on display in the middle of the street.

"Fortunes...?" Before He could keep walking, he heard a man start shouting. He quickly turned toward the source of the noise.

"How many more times are you going to cry!?" The man shouted.

"You're fifteen, for fucks sake!"

Norio realized the noise was coming from inside the tent. He narrowed his eye. There was sobbing, then the man came out of the tent.

"A-Ah...!" He cried as he noticed Norio standing there.

"A-are you awaiting a fortune...?"

Norio smirked.

"Sure am."

The man chuckled nervously.

"Sorry about that, all that noise, please, step inside!"

The man lifted the veil to the tent. Revealing that inside the tent was a young teenage girl.

The girl had lavender hair, twirled in two pigtails, fair skin, and an eye patch on her left eye.

"O-oh! Welcome...!" She greeted, stifling back a sniffle.

"Good fortunes!" The man cried, quickly taking his leave.

"Ah...so you'd like a f-fortune, yes?" She smiled.

Norio sat down on the mat.

"Why not?"

He studied the tent for a minute. *A crystal ball...how cliché.* He thought to himself.

"Uhm...ok!" The girl said, slowly taking off her eye patch.

Norio looked up. The girl's eye that the eye patch covered was white, while her other eye was pink.

"Say," Norio began.

"Yes?" The girl replied.

"What was all that noise about before, you okay?"

The girl quickly looked toward the tent's entrance, then back towards Norio, not making eye contact.

"Mm. I'm fine!" She smiled.

Norio looked at the crystal ball and back at the girl's eye.

"Oi..."

He could continue; the girl cleared her throat.

"Your fortune..." she began.

Norio fell silent.

"You um...you'll lose a loved one, a parent..." she said, shutting her eyes.

Norio quickly looked up.

"What the hell kind of fortune is that-" He stopped himself.

This isn't the girl's fault; she was probably told to spew this kind of bullshit.

"Sorry..." He said, collecting himself.

"Mm, no need." The girl said, looking down steadily.

"You're not the only one; my fortunes are hard to bear for others too."

The girl looked up.

"By the way, my name is Vera!" She smiled.

Norio, who was busy digging for his wallet, nodded.

"Norio." He replied.

"Mm!" She nodded happily.

"How much, Vera?" Vera quickly looked outside the tent.

"Free!" She smiled.

"Hah?"

Vera kept smiling.

"I have a feeling...this won't be the last time we meet, Norio!"

Norio got up.

"That so?" He said as he gave a wave goodbye.

*

After he left, Vera put her eye patch back on.

"Vera Takeshi…" she whispered, smiling to herself.

23 Performance

Keren, who was busy brushing Emersyn's hair, huffed in frustration.

"Why is your hair so thick!?" She cried.

Emersyn pouted.

"Don't be mean to me because Nori got mad at you for oversleeping!" She shouted.

"Hah!? No! your hair is just tough, you brat!" Keren argued.

Norio, busy cooking breakfast, let out a sigh.

He thought about the girl from yesterday.

Weird...

However, before he could finish his thought, he smelled smoke.

"Crap, the eggs!" He quickly took them off the stove.

He turned to the girls.

"Do either of you like overcooked eggs...?"

The girls glared at him in response.

"Guess not..."

*

"Oi, slow down!" Norio cried as Emersyn was tugging him along down the street.

"I can see the circus; hurry up, Keren!" She hollered.

"I'm walking as fast as I can, you brat!" Keren shouted from behind.

"We're here!" Emersyn cried, tugging on Norio's hand.

"Mm." Norio smiled.

As the three walked into the big tent, they got stamped and shown to their seats.

"Nori, can I get a cotton candy!?" Emersyn cried, pointing to the snacks.

"Yeah, sure." They walked toward the counter.

"Yo, get me a popcorn!" Keren hollered.

"Noted!" Norio, due to the loudness, shouted back.

*

"It's about to start!" Emersyn giggled, seated in between the adults.

"See, I can come in handy, you know!" Keren said, giving a triumphant smile.

Then the lights dimmed.

Norio's eye widened as he noticed the man who stepped on stage was yelling at Vera yesterday.

So, this guy is the ringleader...

"Ladies, gentleman, and none of the above!" The ringleader cried out to the audience.

"Are you ready for the main event!?" He cried out.

The audience roared.

"Here we go!"

Canons puffed out colorful smoke, music began playing, and a tiny clown car came to the center of the stage.

*

As the show progressed, Norio kept his eye out in case he saw Vera.

However, she never appeared.

*

As the show came to an end, all the circus members took to the stage and gracefully bowed.

Vera still had not made an appearance.

As the three exited the circus, Keren and Emersyn were busy discussing their favorite parts.

"Hey, what'd you think of the circus, Nori?" Keren smiled over.

"It was okay, I guess."

Keren frowned.

"Oi Oi, don't be such a stick in the mud!" She cried.

Before Norio could retaliate, he bumped into someone.

"Oh, sorry." He looked down to notice Vera, who was sobbing.

She quickly looked up.

"N-Norio...!" She whimpered.

"Oi, Keren, Emmy, I'll be right back!" He shouted back at them as he went to find a desolate spot with Vera.

"Where are y-" Keren's voice faded out.

*

"Now, be open and honest with me; what happened yesterday?" Norio asked, sitting on the ground across from Vera.

Vera sniffled.

"A lot..."

Norio gave a slight smile.

"Clearly." He said, letting out a sigh.

"I was...sold into this circus when I was born," Vera began.

"I was born with the ability to see spirits, and a bit into the future." She frowned.

"My real family gave me up because they didn't want to be 'cursed.'" She looked up at Norio, making sure he was still following along.

"I don't like my abilities; they're...scary." She sniffled.

"What about yesterday...?" Norio asked.

"Your fortune is accurate, sorry."

Norio frowned.

"No, that's not really what I meant," he paused.

"Why was the ringleader mad at you?"

Vera quickly looked up.

"Because...a customer complained about my fortune being inaccurate, and when I went to apologize, she yelled at me and left..." Vera looked down.

"He's not a nice man...he treats all of us like dirt." She narrowed her eyes.

"The circus is just an illusion, we put our fake faces on, and he gets all the glory."

Norio folded his arms.

"Why weren't you there today?"

Vera looked at him.

"Because yesterday, I got banned from being in this town's performance." She smiled sadly.

"Not like I care, though."

Norio nodded.

"I see..." He got up.

Vera's eye widened.

This is the moment he-

"Well, if you're not allowed to perform in the circus, what's the point of you being here?" He smirked.

"Norio..." She looked up.

He extended his hand out.

She sniffled, quickly taking it.

"I know...I know what's about to happen..." She smiled sadly.

"Huh?" He turned.

"You're going to try to get me out of here, but he won't let me..."

Norio cocked his head.

"Who won't let you...?"

Vera laughed nervously.

"The ringleader..."

Norio quickly grabbed her hand.

"I don't care; we have to ask anyway, maybe there's a chance!" He cried.

"C'mon!" He began walking, holding Vera's arm.

Norio, thank you for not taking rejection lightly... She smiled, looking down.

*

"You want to what!?" The ringleader cried.

"What's the point of keeping her here when she's clearly of no use to you!?" Norio angrily shouted.

"Well, she's a great extra-" The man quickly stopped himself.

"A great what, a great extra cash grab!?" Norio cried out.

"That's not what I was going to s-"

Vera glared.

"Yes, it was." She said, staring the ringleader down.

"What's this!?" He began.

"Why are you suddenly being such an ungrateful brat!?" He roared.

"I take you in for all these years, and this is the thanks I get!?" He cried out.

"No, you used me for all these years..." she frowned.

"Give it up, Marx. I already know the outcome; you won't win."

Marx gritted his teeth.

"You have some nerve...!"

He quickly turned to Norio.

"And you!" He shouted.

"Don't think you can come back to our performances; you're banned!" He cried.

"Tch, like I care." Norio huffed, folding his arms.

"Oh no... you'll care when that means you can't see precious little Vera again...!" He smirked.

"Vera, to your room!"

Norio looked up.

"Yes, sir..." She sighed.

"Vera-"

Marx let out a hardy laugh.

"Good, now you...get out of my sight!" He said, pushing Norio out of the tent.

Norio smirked. *Exchanging numbers, acting like this is a dramatic farewell? not bad kid.*

*

"Hah!? Circus costumes!?" Keren cried out.

"Relax," Norio began but was quickly cut off.

"I wanted to be an alien for Halloween, though!" Emersyn cried out.

"Both of you be quiet for a minute!" He sighed.

The girls looked at each other, and then back at him.

"Keren," he began.

"You're flexible, yeah?"

Keren frowned.

"Yeah, I took dance for years; what's your point...?"

Norio smirked.

"Excellent."

24 The Show

Vera woke up from the sound of her alarm going off.

"Showtime..." she smiled.

"Vera." A voice called out.

"Get out here, breakfast."

Vera nodded.

"Coming!" She called out in response.

*

As breakfast progressed, Vera looked at the clock. "Any minute now..."

Marx, reading the newspaper, looked up.

"I have to go..." He quickly got up, his stomach gurgling.

"It's a good thing we're not performing today, huh?" One of the members chuckled.

"Hey, Vera, where are you...?" Vera shushed them and gave a wink.

"To perform on my own!" She waved.

Truth be told, I will never be seeing some of you again; thanks for some good memories... She smiled sadly as she ran.

*

"I hate you." Keren glared at Norio.

"Vera better be worth all of this hassle and embarrassment."

Norio smiled as he finished nailing a sign in.

"Norio!" A voice shouted.

Norio turned around, greeted by Vera.

"Are you ready to do this?"

Vera nodded.

"Mm! I'm a bit rough, but I've had some practice!"

*

"Come one, come all!" Norio shouted out through a megaphone.

"Come to the thrilling, wonderful show, that is the Takeshi family circus!" He cried out.

"H-how much...?" A lady came over to question.

Norio smirked.

"It's for free!" He said, flashing a big grin.

"It's a one-time show." He bowed, reaching behind his back.

He then pulled out a bouquet. The lady was amazed.

 "I'll be there...!" She blushed.

"Isn't there already another circus in town...?" A man asked as he began to walk away; Keren jumped in front of him.

"That's right, but this circus is free, free, free!" She cried out.

The man jumped.

"I'll...think about it." He muttered, continuing his way.

"Nori?" Emersyn asked.

"Hah?"

Emersyn looked at him.

"How do we know if people are actually going to come...like for sure?"

Norio smiled.

"False hope." He answered, petting Emersyn's head.

"Just keep pulling that flower crap; the chicks are digging it." Keren giggled.

*

Norio clapped his hands together.

"'Kay, are you guys ready?"

Keren looked up from her phone.

"I guess…"

Norio turned to Emersyn. She, in turn, pouted.

"I'm not even allowed to do anything!" She folded her arms.

Norio ran his fingers through his hair and sighed.

"Would letting you sit on a canon, please you?"

Emersyn quickly turned.

"Yes!?" She cried.

You better hold on tight then." He grumbled.

"Oi, Vera," he turned to her.

"Are you ready?"

Vera looked up.

"Mm, I just...get a bit of stage fright usually, b-but I'm fine...!" She smiled.

Norio nodded.

"Okay, let's do this." He grinned.

*

Keren peaked her head out from a curtain.

"Waah...there's a lot more people who showed up than I expected..." she sighed, turning to Norio.

"You ready to bullshit this...?"

Norio nodded.

"Don't mess this up." The pair said in unison, smirking at each other.

*

The lights dimmed.

"Yahoo!" Emersyn cried; as a canon, she sat on top of fired-out purple and pink smoke.

"Ladies, and gentlemen, boys and girls, and none of the above!" A voice called out from the shadows.

"Are you ready!?"

The audience looked around in confusion.

"Let's get it!"

Suddenly, Norio came back flipping out onto the stage. Music began playing, and the audience roared.

Norio whipped his whip.

"I'd like to thank you all for coming; we have a fantastic show for you guys today!" He grinned.

"Now introducing, our lovely Acrobatics, Keren, and Vera!"

The audience cheered.

Vera stood on the catwalk nervously.

"Just remember," Norio told her.

"Keren will be doing most of the acrobatics. All you have to do is catch her, and she'll pull you to her side of the catwalk."

Vera gave a nod as she remembered.

Because I have my eye patch on, I can't see what happens next, but I trust you, Norio! She thought to herself.

Keren waved to the audience and struck a pose.

"We got this..." She whispered to herself.

Keren then did a flip into the air, grabbing the swing.

I did it...!

"Oh, thank god..." Norio whispered to himself.

Emersyn looked up in amazement.

Get ready...! Now! Vera twirled around, waving to the audience.

The audience kept cheering.

As Keren flew over, she extended her arms; Vera quickly grabbed on.

"How's it going?" Keren whispered.

"Y-you did amazing, Keren...!" Vera whispered, amazed.

As the two landed back onto Keren's side, they waved to the audience, with Keren blowing a kiss.

"Give it up for the amazing, Keren and Vera!" Norio cried out.

The audience roared.

*

As the show came to an end, the four members bowed to the audience.

*

"How the heck did we do it..." Keren said, looking around at the now-empty building.

"Don't know, but my bank account is crying." Norio sighed.

"Renting this place out last minute probably wasn't the best move..."

Vera giggled.

Suddenly, a voice boomed out from the entrance.

"You!"

They all quickly turned.

It was Marx.

"Who is that old bald dude...?" Keren pointed.

Norio glared.

"Show's over, I'm afraid," Norio said.

Marx came barreling down the steps in a rage.

"Why did you do all of this!?"

Norio grinned.

"Oh, you know, for the laughs." He replied.

Marx gritted his teeth.

"Wh-"

Norio quickly cut him off.

"I think you know why, Marx."

He said as he gave a glance towards Vera.

"For that!?" Marx cried out.

"Fine! Fucks sake, take her!" Marx shouted.

"She's no use to me anymore!" He cried.

"Under one condition!"

Norio raised an eyebrow.

"Hoh...? Care to tell me what that one condition is?" He smirked.

"Never! Pull this shit," he gestured to the room.

"Again!"

Norio closed his eye and nodded.

"I see, I see, noted, sir!" He smiled.

Marx glared at Vera.

"Ungrateful little..." He muttered as he stormed off.

Norio waved.

*

"Ok, well, I'm starving." Norio began.

"We probably can't afford anything decent now," Keren grumbled.

"Oi, I'm not that broke, dummy." He frowned.

Vera giggled.

"I like you guys!" She beamed.

Norio smiled.

"Ah, that's good."

*

As they reached the exit, they noticed a pink-haired man standing outside.

The man began clapping.

"That was quite the show!" He smiled.

Norio smiled.

"Thanks, I mean, it's been over, but I'm glad you stuck around to tell us that."

The man beamed.

"I'd love to see you perform one day again!" The man laughed.

"Sorry, But that's not going to h-"

Before Norio could finish, the man began walking away.

"My favorite part was the clown, by the way!"

Emersyn pointed at herself in astonishment and beamed.

Norio ran his fingers through his hair.

"Anyways," he said as the four of them continued walking together.

*

The next morning, Rick flipped the page of the newspaper. The column on that read, 'One-time circus success.'

Rick studied the picture for a few moments.

"There's no way..." He chuckled, getting up.

The picture displayed a man dressed up as a ringleader, dark blue hair, and a bandage over his face's right side.

25 Disguised

"Bring your kid to work day...?" Rick looked up.

"Mm!" Tammy nodded enthusiastically.

"You should bring Maru!"

Rick turned around and sighed.

 "How many times do I have to say that Maru isn't my-"

Then, there was a knock at the door.

"Oh, you're both still here...?" Ms. Hoffman asked, peeking her head in.

"Y-yeah!" Rick exclaimed.

Ms. Hoffman smiled.

"Annette, tomorrow is bring your kid to work day, right?" Tammy asked.

Ms. Hoffman nodded.

"Mm, it sure is."

She turned to Rick.

"Did I just hear you have a kid?"

Rick quickly looked at Tammy, then back to Ms. Hoffman.

"Y-Yea, her name is Maru!" He smiled nodding.

"I see, well, don't be shy. I'd love to meet her." She smiled.

"Later." She said, leaving.

"Hey, I should get home-" Rick began.

Tammy glared.

"What's that look for...?"

Tammy let out a sigh.

"You're hopeless; I'll see you later," Tammy huffed as she left.

What the heck did I do... Rick sighed.

*

"Really!?" Maru exclaimed.

"Yep, plus, my students are around your age; maybe you'll make friends!" He smiled, handing Maru a backpack.

Maru gave a big smile.

*

"Good morning, class," Rick began.

"I'd like you all to meet my kid, Maru!" He smiled.

"Wave, Maru." He whispered.

Maru looked up at him nervously, then waved.

"Mr. Summers?" A girl asked.

"Yes, Sasha?" Rick answered.

"How old is Maru?"

Rick looked at Maru.

"I don't know, ask her."

Maru looked back and forth for a second.

 "I'm almost six...!"

Sasha smiled.

"Me too!" She giggled.

Maru gave a big smile.

*

"Do you want to sit with the kids or me?" Rick asked, carrying a tray of food.

"I'll be sitting with the adults."

Maru looked around the cafeteria.

Before she could answer, Sasha ran over.

"Mr. Summers, can Maru sit with us!?" She cried.

Rick laughed.

"Ask her."

Sasha quickly turned to Maru.

"Want to sit with us!?"

Maru nodded.

"Mm!"

Sasha quickly grabbed her hand.

"C'mon!" The girls giggled as they went over to the table.

Rick smiled as he watched.

"Mr. Summers?" Ms. Hoffman tapped him on the shoulder.

Rick jumped.

"A-Ah hi!" He quickly turned.

"Where's Maru...?"

Rick looked over toward the table.

"Ah, sorry she's eating with my class..."

Ms. Hoffman nodded.

"Introduce us later, okay?" She smiled.

Rick quickly nodded.

*

As lunch ended, the class went back to the classroom.

"Ok, don't think you kids are off from doing any work!" Rick grinned, pulling out a box.

The kids groaned.

"What's that?" Maru asked, pointing.

"Clay, they're making some boats." He smiled.

"Ooh!" Maru gave a nod.

*

The kids began lining up to get onto their buses.

Rick waved goodbye to the kids as they filed out, led by Tammy.

"Oh!" Rick exclaimed, turning to Maru.

Maru looked up from coloring.

"Mm?" She cocked her head.

"There's a nice lady, and she wants to meet you!" Rick smiled.

Maru blushed.

"Really?" She asked.

As the two walked over towards Ms. Hoffman's classroom, they noticed Sasha and her mother.

"Oh, Maru!" Sasha said, running over to them.

"Want to be my friend!?" She smiled.

Maru blushed.

"Mm!" She smiled, giving a hard nod.

"Mr. Summers, I've heard so many nice things about you."

Rick turned around.

"Ah, Sasha's mom." He smiled.

"Your daughter is a great student."

Sasha's mother smiled.

"That's great to hear."

Sasha tugged at her mother's arm.

"Mm?" Her Mother bent down.

"Can we exchange phone numbers...?" Sasha whispered.

"Oh, of course." Her mother smiled.

"Sasha would like to exchange numbers with Maru. Is that alright...?" She asked.

"Oh yeah, sure!" Rick smiled.

As he finished writing the digits down, he handed it to Sasha's mother.

"Thank you very much; we'll keep in touch." Sasha's mom smiled as they waved goodbye.

Then, Ms. Hoffman stepped into her doorway.

Her eyes widened.

"Is that..." she began.

"Oh! Ms. Hoffman, this is Maru!" Rick smiled.

Maru turned around.

Ms. Hoffman looked shocked momentarily but quickly brushed it off.

"Maru, it's...nice to meet you." She smiled. Maru looked up at her and nodded.

"Thank you..." Maru whispered.

As Rick waved goodbye, Ms. Hoffman turned the lights off in her classroom.

She narrowed her eyes.

"I knew it..."

26 Six

"Hey," Chris greeted as Rick walked in the door.

"Hey, thanks a ton for babysitting." Rick smiled.

"Nah, no problem dude, 'sides, she fell asleep," Chris said, pointing to the couch with Maru fast asleep on it.

"By the way," Chris began.

"I wanted to tell you; I went digging for her files," he paused.

"Her Birthday is in like, three days."

Rick quickly looked up.

"Eh!?" He cried.

Chris quickly raised a finger to shush him.

"Yeah, according to her file, it's on the 17th of October."

Rick looked around frantically.

"I don't have time, I mean, I really don't have time to put together a party an-"

Chris shot him a look.

"Yeah, and that's where the four of us come in!" He smirked.

"The huh...?" Rick asked, giving a confused smile.

"Sena, Tammy, Abbey, and I, duh!" Rick sighed.

"I see..." He whispered.

"Don't worry, your pretty little blonde head none!" Chris laughed.

"We'll take care of it."

Rick looked at him.

"You will...?" He sighed in relief.

"Wait," Rick turned his head to look at Maru.

"Does...she even know her birthday?"

Chris stretched his arms behind his head.

"I don't know; just tell her, I guess in case."

Chris looked at his watch.

"Well, I have to go; I'll keep in touch with you." He said, standing up.

"Chris..." Rick said, hugging him.

"Thank you."

Chris blushed, awkwardly embracing him back.

*

"My birthday...?"

Rick nodded his head.

"Do you know when it is?"

Maru frowned.

"I don't know..."

Rick smiled, patting her head.

"Don't worry, that's perfectly fine."

Maru gave a smile.

"Do you know...?" She asked.

Rick turned.

"According to your fi- Chris," he corrected himself.

"It's in two days."

Maru quickly sat up.

"Really!?"

"Mm!" Rick nodded.

Maru's eyes twinkled.

"I'm going to be six!" She cried.

Rick smiled, watching her get so excited.

"Um..." she looked down sheepishly.

"Mm?" Rick bent down.

"Can I have cheesecake...?" She looked up at Rick, blushing.

Rick couldn't help but laugh.

"Well, yeah, why not?" He laughed.

Maru looked down again quickly.

"You're nice to me..." She raised her head.

"I love you!" She grinned.

Rick blushed.

"You deserve a nice birthday." He said, stroking her head.

*

"Rick!"

Tammy cried from the living room.

"Yo?" Rick looked up quickly from the cheesecake he was preparing.

"Sena wants to know, what is Maru's favorite color?" Rick thought about it for a second.

"Purple, I'm pretty sure!"

Tammy nodded.

"Got it!" She said, jotting it down on a checklist.

"Ok," Chris began.

"I invited Sasha, her mother, Sena, Abbey, Tammy," He paused.

"Is there anyone I'm missing?" He asked, turning to Rick.

"Nope, I think that covers everyone." He said.

"Ok, cool, I also got the balloons." He turned.

"Also," he began.

"A few presents, from me," he said, pointing to a pile of wrapped gifts.

"Chris!?" Rick cried.

Chris chuckled.

"No, I mean, I appreciate it," Rick began.

"But where the hell am I going to put all of it!?" He cried.

Chris frowned.

"Relax, you'll find space."

Rick let out a sigh.

"I better." He mumbled.

*

Rick looked at the clock nervously.

Everyone would be arriving soon, including Maru, who was out all day with Sena, and Abbey.

He sighed, planting a party hat on his head.

Suddenly, there was a knock at the door. Rick sprang up.

"Oh, Sasha!" He smiled.

"Hi, Mr. Summers!" She beamed.

"My mom told me to say that she had work, but appreciated you inviting her anyway!" She said.

"Ah, that's fine; I'm glad you're here, at least."

Sasha nodded.

"Mm!" She giggled.

The door suddenly slammed open. Chris came in, carrying a bunch of games.

"Oi, watch my door." Rick scolded.

"Sorry, sorry," Chris grumbled.

"You know," Rick began.

"I think you're even more worked up about this whole thing than I am."

Chris chuckled.

"That so?"

Tammy came next.

"They're not here yet...?" She looked around.

"Hi, Ms. Pembroke!" Sasha shouted from across the room.

"Sasha!" Tammy smiled, waving.

Rick sighed.

"Nope, they're not here yet." He folded his arms.

"Relax," Chris began.

Before he could finish, Abbey peaked her head in the doorway.

"Oh crap," she said, noticing everyone was already there.

"Language," Chris said.

"Shut it, Huser." Abbey huffed, walking in.

"Oh!" Sena exclaimed, laughing nervously.

"I picked out some flowers." She smiled.

"Come on in, birthday girl!" She beamed.

Maru came walking in sheepishly.

Everyone began clapping.

"Oh! Sasha!" Maru cried out, noticing the girl.

"Maru!" Sasha ran over. The two embraced; the adults laughed.

*

As the day went on, they played games and held various conversations.

Next, it was time for presents.

"Maru, want to open mine first?" Sasha asked.

"Mm!" Maru nodded.

Maru unwrapped the present and smiled.

"What did you get?" Rick asked, leaning over.

Maru held up a coloring book and gave a big smile.

"Thank you!" Maru beamed, hugging her friend.

"My turn!" Chris said.

Rick pushed him back.

"You'll go last, rich boy." He said.

Chris gave a sad nod.

"Well," Tammy began.

She pulled out a present from behind her.

"I guess I'll go next!" She said, handing Maru the present.

"Thank you, Tammy!" Maru smiled.

Maru opened the present and gasped.

"Bead bracelets!" She cried in amazement.

Tammy knelt beside her.

"I used to make these all the time as a kid; I thought you'd like it!" She smiled.

Maru hugged her quickly, causing Tammy to grunt.

"Thank you, Tammy!" She cried, hugging her.

"Now's our turn." Abbey smiled.

"Sena and I got a joint gift; hope that's ok."

"Mm!" Maru said, giving a hard nod.

They walked over, holding a giant teddy bear.

Rick did his best suppressing a groan.

"Happy birthday!" They said in unison, handing her the bear.

Maru's face lit up.

"Thank you!" She cried in amazement.

"It's even bigger than her..." Chris said, nudging Rick.

"I don't even want to think about it," Rick whispered.

As the gift-giving ended, with various toys from Chris, they sang happy birthday and gave the cake.

"You made this!?" Maru cried.

"Yup!" Rick nodded, smiling sheepishly.

*

As the party came to an end, everyone said their goodbyes.

"Thank you, guys," Rick said, waving as they all left.

Maru sat up, waking up from sleeping on the couch.

"They left...?" She questioned tiredly.

Rick nodded, sitting beside her, stroking her hair.

"Did you have fun?" He smiled.

Maru nodded, laying on him.

"Thank you, Rick." She gave an exhausted smile.

"Looks like you're ready for bed." He said, getting up.

"Rick...?" Maru called out.

"Mm?" He turned.

"Can I lay with you?" She asked.

Rick looked over at his bed.

"Why not." He smiled.

*

With Maru lying on him, Rick laid down with her hands on his chest, staring at the ceiling.

Is this really ok...? Is someone like me allowed to have this? Am I really allowed a second chance at happiness...?

He looked down at Maru on top of him, running his fingers through her hair.

He smiled sadly. *As selfish as it may be, I don't want this to end...* He thought as he dozed off.

27 Richie Rich

"Hey," Rick began, as he walked over to the couch.

"What's up?" Chris asked.

"While I do appreciate the unnecessary amount of presents you got for Maru," he paused, then smirked.

"Oi, Oi, what are you smirking about?" Chris glared.

"You're a Richie rich, aren't you?" He asked snidely.

Chris blushed then quickly turned away.

"Nah, I just came into good money at the time, is all." He responded.

Rick narrowed his eyes.

"Really, for when you failed at kidnapping Maru?" He taunted.

Chris shot Rick a look.

"What the hell are you trying to get at!?" He cried.

"Nothing," Rick paused.

"Abbey found something interesting about you, though."

Chris turned his head.

"What?"

Rick handed Chris his phone.

"Give us a tour?" He grinned.

"How did you find my house!?" Chris cried, just as Abbey stepped into the apartment.

"Quit yelling, idiot." Abbey sighed, placing a hand on her hip.

"I was curious as to how you got so many gifts, so I... did some digging." She turned away to hide a smirk.

"Don't you have anything better to do!?" He then turned his attention to Rick, who was sneering.

"What!?" He growled.

"Nothing, nothing!" Rick paused.

"We just think it's cute that you're a...rich boy; that's all."

Abbey snickered.

"Oh, relax, will you?" She said.

Chris grumbled.

"It's my dad's business; I'm just the heir." Chris then turned.

"Besides, why is this so funny to both of you?"

Rick and Abbey looked at each other.

"Well," Rick began.

"I don't care about money, or whatever," he began.

"I don't know; I just want to live normally."

Rick and Abbey burst out laughing.

"Relax, we're not persecuting you for being rich, as I said, we-"

Before Rick could finish, Chris shot him a look.

"I know I'm well off; you don't have to say it twice," he began.

"My point is, people, use me for my money; I haven't," he looked away, blushing.

"Made any real friends since...you guys." He sighed.

"That's why I didn't want to tell you..."

Rick grumbled, scratching his head.

Abbey looked down.

"Sorry..." The two mumbled in unison.

"I mean, if you want-" He stopped.

Rick looked up.

"What?"

Chris looked steadily down.

"What were you going to say?" Rick asked frowning.

"If you want to come over..." Chris blushed.

Rick and Abbey exchanged looks.

Abbey sighed.

"Not after the way we just treated you." She scratched her neck.

"We were childish and unfair."

She looked up at Chris.

"Sorry."

Chris smiled sadly.

"Nah, don't worry. I understand it's funny."

Rick turned to Abbey.

"I have to go, but I'll see you." She turned to leave.

"Listen up, idiot," she looked at Chris.

"I'm going to say it once…" She looked away.

"Don't you ever forget we really care about you." She looked down, blushing.

"B-Bye." She quickly shut the door.

Chris gave a smile.

"No, shit."

Rick let out a yawn and stretched.

"We'll try better next time." He smiled, patting Chris on the shoulder.

*

"Master," a voice called out.

"Master," the voice repeated.

Chris stirred.

"You have guests, master Chris."

Chris yawned, rising in his bed.

"What is it, pops?" He asked, rubbing his eyes.

"You have guests, master." The man repeated.

Chris shot up.

"What!?" He cried.

"Hobbes, why didn't you wake me sooner!?" He cried.

Hobbes looked at him.

"Master, they just c-"

Chris started flinging around his clothes frantically.

"I have to go get dressed!" He cried.

Chris kept pressing the elevator button frantically.

"This must be an important client if they're here so early." He grumbled.

As the elevator came, he quickly stepped inside. He began fixing his scarf.

As he stepped out of the elevator, one of his maids turned.

"Yo!" She greeted.

"Your guests are in the guest room."

Chris nodded.

"Shouldn't you be working extra hard then?" He asked, giving an irritated grin.

The girl looked up from her phone.

"Nah." She replied, turning her attention back to her phone.

"Ema..." Chris growled.

"Relax!" She said, getting up.

"They don't seem all too bad." Ema began.

"Besides, don't stress, I don't want to see you bald." She shuddered.

"Ew, I need to get that image out of my head..." She grumbled as she walked away.

"That girl..." Chris grumbled.

He checked the mirror quickly. He then began fixing his hair.

"What am I doing? I don't have time for this!" He cried, slamming open the doors to the guest room.

"I'm so sorry, I-"

When he opened his eyes, he was greeted by Rick, Maru, Sena, Abbey, and Tammy.

"Eh!?" He cried out.

"They felt bad for their poor behavior yesterday," Sena frowned.

"Sena…" Abbey quickly blushed.

"Mm, plus, we wanted to make up for it by bringing you a gift!" Tammy smiled, holding up a bottle of wine.

"You don't need to do any of that; don't be sorry either." Chris sighed, scratching his head.

"You could have just warned me, you know." He looked up, then noticed Ema and Hobbes peeking their heads in.

"H-hey…!" He stammered.

"D-don't just stand there; you two have jobs!" He cried.

They then walked into the room.

"Relax, dummy, my job, as you said, was to get you some coffee." She said, placing a tray with cups of coffee onto the table.

"Since when do you expect us to do our jobs? You're never this bossy!" She grumbled.

"I had to learn how to make coffee, you big jerk!" She placed her hands on her hips.

"Thanks, Ema, Hobbes, you two can leave now." He said while gritting his teeth.

"But," Ema began.

"I said you could leave now." He repeated.

"Relax, we're not bothering anyone, right?" She smiled, looking at his friends.

"Nah, she's fine," Rick replied.

Ema smiled, bowing her dress.

"So, what did you guys want to do...?" Chris chuckled nervously.

Maru looked up at Rick.

"I'm hungry..."

Rick turned to Chris.

"If it's not a bother-"

Chris quickly got up.

"It's not; I'll go get her something!" He said as he left the room.

 "How's this, shrimp?" He walked back in, holding up a package of chocolate-covered biscuits.

Maru's eyes twinkled.

"Really!?" She cried.

They all laughed as Chris handed the packet to Maru.

*

After a couple of hours, the group said their goodbyes and left.

Chris hummed as he walked back to the elevator.

As the elevator came down the shaft, he beamed.

I finally have true friends... He thought to himself, smiling as he stepped into the elevator.

28 Date

Rick let out a sigh as he packed up his belongings. The school day had come to an end.

As he was walking down the hall, Ms. Hoffman tapped his shoulder from behind. Startled, he jumped.

"Oh...sorry, I didn't mean to scare you." She looked at him, then quickly looked down.

"N-Nah, it's fine! Is everything ok...?" He chuckled nervously.

Ms. Hoffman began blushing.

"M-Ms. Hoffman...?" Rick whispered, hesitantly touching her shoulder.

"Are you okay...?"

She looked up, blushing wildly.

"Will you go on a date with me, Mr. Summers!?" She cried out.

Rick nearly fell.

Quickly becoming a blushing mess, too.

"M-me!?" He cried.

Ms. Hoffman nodded, averting her eyes.

"I-I'd love to!" He stammered.

Ms. Hoffman quickly looked up.

"R-really?" She smiled, tearing up.

She then leaned on Rick's chest.

"I've always...wanted you." She whispered as she slid a finger up near the right side of his collar bone.

"W-we shouldn't do this in a school zone..." Rick stammered, looking around frantically in case anyone was witnessing this scene.

Ms. Hoffman slowly rose.

"I'll meet you at the Italian restaurant, Ciarlatano..." she gave a smile.

"By the way, please call me Annette." She said, wiping a tear.

Rick stood up.

"A-ah, and you can call me Rick if you want!" He laughed, scratching his head.

Annette nodded.

"I'll see you later!" Rick waved, turning toward the door, leaving.

Ms. Hoffman smiled as she waved.

*

"A date...?" Chris asked, holding up a suit.

"Why, are you jealous?" Rick laughed.

Chris frowned.

"The hell I am!"

He then looked around the room for a minute.

"I mean, it's just...sudden, I guess."

Rick smiled as Chris handed him the suit.

"Relax, it's just a date; I doubt it'll be anything serious," he paused.

"I've had a huge crush on her; I really didn't think she'd notice me."

Chris sighed, scratching his head.

"What's her name?" He asked.

"Annette Hoffman," Rick replied, fixing his collar.

"Why does that sound...familiar," Chris said, biting his lip in thought.

"It's a popular last name, I guess." Rick smiled, turning around.

"How do I look?" He asked.

Chris laughed.

"Like a try-hard idiot." He smiled, looking down.

"You're a good person, Rick."

Rick chuckled. "I don't want to hear something like that about a person like me."

Chris gave a sad smile, patting his shoulder.

"Go get them." He said.

"Alright, I'm off!" Rick shouted.

Maru quickly ran out of his bedroom.

"Wait!" She cried.

"Give this to her!" She shouted, holding up a beaded bracelet.

Rick knelt.

"Sure." He smiled, ruffling her hair. As he got up, he waved to Chris, and Maru then left.

*

Annette studied herself in a mirror, then let out a long sigh.

"You can do this..." She reassured herself.

"Cole..." She whispered.

She smiled sadly as she tucked away a photograph into her purse.

29 Revenge

As the cab arrived at the restaurant, Rick stepped out. He began fixing his tie, then smoothing his hair.

"Ok!" He smiled as he walked in. He began looking around the restaurant, searching for Annette.

Someone then tapped him on the shoulder. Startled, he quickly spun around.

Rick was met with Annette, wearing a spaghetti strap green dress.

"A-Annette!" He yelped.

"Did I scare you again...?" She smiled, reaching for his hand.

Rick held her hand and smiled.

"Shall we?" Rick asked.

Annette giggled.

"Let's."

*

"Chris?" A voice called out from behind the door.

Chris opened the door, greeted by Tammy.

"Oh, Tammy!" Chris smiled.

"I came to see if you needed any help with watching Maru," She began as she looked over at the couch which Maru was fast asleep on.

Tammy smiled softly.

"Actually," Chris looked at her.

"You and Rick's date are also coworkers, right?"

Tammy gave a nod.

"What's up?" She asked, looking at Chris's computer.

"Nothing, I'm just..." He quickly paused.

Tammy leaned in closer.

"What's wrong?"

Chris froze.

"Chris...?"

"Holy shit, we need to get to that restaurant right now." He cried, quickly grabbing Tammy's arm.

"I'll explain in the car; we have to go!" He shouted as the two rushed out the door.

*

"Actually," Annette looked at Rick, who was seated across from her.

"Yeah?"

Annette giggled.

"I'm not actually...hungry." She smiled.

Rick blushed heavily as he noticed her tugging on one of her straps.

*

"I knew Hoffman sounded familiar, shit!" Chris cried, slamming the car door shut.

"Basically," he began.

"Let's go somewhere...private." Annette smiled, walking over toward Rick.

Rick rose quickly.

*

"She was the aunt of a patient," he paused.

"His name was Cole Hoffman, also known as 245."

Tammy nodded anxiously.

*

"Just the two of us..." she said as she guided him towards the restrooms.

*

"245 was killed by a new doctor in the department..."

*

As they got in the bathroom, Annette locked the door from the inside.

"Wouldn't want anyone to ruin the fun." She winked.

Rick looked at her purse, then quickly back up at her as he leaned against the wall.

"Mm, wouldn't want that." He grinned.

*

"The Reaper," Chris looked at Tammy, who was covering her mouth in disbelief.

"You mean..."

*

"The truth is," Annette began, as she walked over toward Rick.

"I've been waiting for this moment for a while..." she said as she pinned one arm above him.

"Really now?" Rick asked, his eyes narrowing.

*

As their cab pulled up to the restaurant, they ran in quickly.

"Call the cops, now!" Chris shouted.

*

Annette nodded, reaching slowly into her purse.

"I wanted to thank you...Mr. Reaper." She said, her voice going cold.

"Thank you...for taking everything from me..."

*

After a few moments, Annette still stood there frozen, staring steadily down at the man. A knife jammed in his right shoulder.

"Tch, you didn't even flinch." She frowned.

Rick sat there, staring down at the floor.

Suddenly, there was a banging on the door.

Annette looked up quickly as she heard Tammy screaming.

Chris was frantically trying to break down the door.

She threw down the photo she had in her purse toward Rick.

Rick stared weakly at the photograph.

The door came off its hinges.

"Rick!" Tammy cried as the two ran toward him.

The police quickly handcuffed Annette.

As they took her away, she kept her gaze steadily down.

"Rick!" Chris cried, frantically grabbing his face.

Relax you, idiot, I can hear you just fine... Rick thought to himself as everything faded to black.

30 Bonds

There was a buzz of commotion. Monitors beeping, IVs dripping.

Rick began stirring. He sat up clumsily.

Looking around, he let out a sigh.

"I'm alive..." he muttered.

He looked around the hospital room.

Suddenly, a nurse came walking over.

"Ah, Mr. Summers, you're awake!" She gave a smile.

Rick gave a nod.

"Your friends are out right now but said they'd be back soon." She paused.

"Is there anything I can get you?"

Rick shook his head.

The nurse smiled sadly.

"Not in the mood to talk, I see." She said, walking away.

*

As Rick was eating some pudding, there was a knock on the door.

The door opened as Chris walked in.

"Yo." He gave a wave.

He quickly sat on the stool next to the bed.

"Get me the hell out of here."

Chris scratched his head.

"Geez, not even a hello, huh?"

"Seriously," Rick said, narrowing his eyes.

Chris huffed as he clapped his hands on his knees.

"The doctors said you're doing swimmingly; I'm sure you'll be out of here soon."

Rick sighed.

"Tammy's at school, so she couldn't make it; she apologizes."

Rick looked out the window.

"Is that so?" He said, not taking his gaze off the outdoors.

"The sun is bright." He said.

"Really, I had no idea." Chris snickered.

Rick laid back a bit.

"Where are Sena and Abbey?" He asked.

"Watching your kid."

Rick frowned, then bit his lip.

"What?" Chris looked at him.

"You look like you have something to say."

Rick turned back toward the window.

"How's Annette...?"

Chris looked down for a minute.

"They placed her in a mental asylum."

Rick quickly looked up.

"Huh!?" He cried.

"She didn't do anything, though!"

Chris looked at him.

"Rick she-"

Rick glared.

"In fact, I don't think I ever asked for your involvement."

Chris folded his arms and huffed.

"If I hadn't helped you, you could have seriously gotten hurt, maybe not a near-death situation, but-"

Rick laughed.

Chris looked stunned as Rick continued to laugh.

"Maybe it's what I deserved." He said, wiping a tear.

"I took the one thing, the one person that meant the world to her."

He looked down.

"Give her a break, will you?"

Chris looked steadily at the floor.

"If none of this happened, Maru wouldn't have come into your life," he paused.

"And you wouldn't have come into ours."

Rick fell silent.

"Who's?"

Chris shot him a look.

"Don't play dumb; you know I meant Sena, Abbey, Tammy's, and mine."

Rick kept looking down.

"Am I really that worth it to you people?"

Chris didn't answer.

"Cole, and especially Maru, would have been much better off without me."

Chris's hand slowly formed a fist.

"I shouldn't have taken that fuckin' job-"

Before he could finish, Chris slugged him hard across the face.

Rick's eyes widened.

Chris's fist shook.

"Do you hear yourself..." He looked down.

"Do you hear what you're saying?" His fist shook harder.

"If you didn't take that job, both of them would've ended up dead."

Chris began shaking.

"Both of those innocent kids, they would have never lasted in that place, that's why...!" He looked up at Rick.

"That's why it's your job; it's your job to keep your damn promise!" He cried.

"Keep your promise, not only for that kids' sake but for Maru's sake!" He shouted.

"You're right; Maru deserves better," he paused.

"That's why," he shook.

"That's why you're in her life, that's why..."

His voice cracked.

"That's why you're in all of our lives..." He smiled as tears fell.

Rick looked at him, stunned.

"Chris..." He said, touching his cheek.

"Don't fucking punch me like that again, you jerk!" He cried.

"Give me a warning, at least!"

Chris's eyes widened. Through his tears, he began laughing.

"You're really one of a kind." He smiled.

Rick smiled, looking up at him.

"Thank you, Chris."

Chris nodded.

"That's what friends are for."

Rick closed his eyes, nodding.

"That's what friends are for." He repeated.

31 Brothers

"Rick!" A voice cried out.

As Rick walked into the door of their apartment, Maru charged at him, hugging his waist.

Rick grunted at the force.

She began sobbing.

Rick gave a sad smile as he patted Maru on the head.

Sena walked out of the bedroom.

"Welcome home, Rick." She smiled softly.

"You didn't...you know, tell her exactly what happened, right?" Rick asked as he sat on the couch.

Sena shook her head.

"All we told her was that you got sick."

Rick nodded his head.

"I see."

Sena stared at her lap in silence for a minute.

"How are you?" She whispered.

Rick looked at her and then looked away.

"Fine, I guess..." He mumbled.

Sena kept her gaze shifted down.

"Rick..." She then fell silent.

"Huh?"

Sena smiled sadly.

"Someone...came to my shop."

Rick turned to her.

"A man, he claimed to be your brother."

Rick's eyes widened.

"He gave me instructions," before she could finish, Rick began to tremble.

"Rick...?" She asked, concerned.

"He's okay..."

Sena looked at him, confused.

"Rick," she said, as she slipped a piece of paper onto his lap.

"Those are his instructions..." Sena whispered.

Rick quickly opened the crumpled paper. His eyes darted as he read the contents of the paper.

He then slowly lowered the paper.

"Meet up with him on my birthday..."

Sena looked at him.

"Your birthday is December sixteenth...?" She asked, then looked down shyly.

"I only read the paper in case I lost it..." she confessed sheepishly.

"Sena," Rick began.

"Hm?" She looked up.

"How was he...?" Rick paused.

"How 's Norio?"

32 Fourteen

As the sunrise came, Norio sat on the porch watching.

Then came a tap on his shoulder. He turned around, greeted by Keren.

"Mind if I sit?" She smiled.

"Go ahead." He replied.

She plopped down beside him.

"So..." she began.

Norio kept his sight on the sun as it rose.

"You think you found him, huh?"

Norio kept looking forward.

"Mm."

Keren smiled.

"Are you nervous?" She asked.

Norio looked at her.

"Why should I be?" Keren turned.

"I don't know; you haven't seen him in what, thirteen years?"

Norio looked down.

"It's been fourteen, but-" He cut himself off.

"But...?" She looked at him.

"Nori," Keren frowned.

"Sun's up; I'll go make some breakfast," Norio said as he got up and stretched.

Keren watched as he walked inside and let out a sigh.

*

"You didn't know?" Chris asked as he took a seat on one of the stools in the kitchenette.

"How would I?" Rick frowned.

"I didn't work there very long," he then paused.

"The hell would he be doing in a place like that anyway..."

Chris let out a sigh, placing a hand on his chin.

"Beats me." He looked at his phone.

"Nervous?"

Rick looked up at him.

"Why would I be?"

Chris shrugged.

"Just wondering."

Rick looked down.

"Well...it's been fourteen years," He paused.

"I guess...I'm just a bit nervous." He admitted.

"Why?"

Rick gave him a look.

"The hell do you mean, why?"

Chris grinned.

"B-because..." Rick looked down, blushing.

"What if he grew taller than me," he paused.

"Or, what if..."

Chris cocked his head.

"Nothing, never mind." He sighed.

"Quit being so nosy, Chris."

Chris chuckled.

"You're right, my bad."

Rick looked towards his bedroom door.

"'Sides," he began.

"Wonder what he'll think of Maru."

Chris nodded.

"I see." He said.

*

The next couple of days flew by.

"Hey," Chris greeted, stepping into the door.

"Happy birthday, old man." He smiled.

Rick laughed.

"Thanks, but I'm not nearly as old as you."

Chris chuckled.

"Be nice to your elders, you punk."

Chris looked over at the clock on the wall.

"What time did the instructions say...?"

Rick took the paper out of his pants pocket.

"Around the evening." Rick said.

"You sure you don't mind watching Maru?"

Chris nodded.

"Of course. Why would I?"

Rick smiled.

"I don't know, just checking."

Suddenly, Maru ran out of the bedroom.

"Rick!" She cried.

The men turned their attention to her.

"Look, it's done!" She cried, holding up two bracelets triumphantly.

"They look awesome, kiddo." He smiled.

Chris nodded.

"Nice job, shrimp!"

Maru beamed, handing Rick the bracelets.

"This one is yours," she pointed at the yellow one.

"And this," she said, pointing at the purple one.

"Is..." She frowned.

"Norio's?"

Maru quickly nodded.

"Mm!"

Rick smiled, patting her on the head.

"Happy birthday, Rick!" Maru exclaimed, hugging him.

Rick looked at Chris.

Chris gave him a look.

Then, Rick knelt on a knee and embraced Maru.

"You're a great kid, Maru."

Maru blushed.

"Thank you so much." He whispered as he hugged her.

"Mm!" She beamed as he got up.

*

As Rick was leaving, Maru quickly ran over.

"Tell him I said hi!" She said.

Rick gave a nod.

"Roger!" He smiled.

"Bye!" She said as she and Chris waved.

*

As Rick shut the door, he let out a sigh and walked toward his cab.

*

"Tsk, he forgot the instructions," Chris said, picking up the paper.

"Hm?" He stared at it for a good second.

"I shouldn't..."

He looked around. Then he quickly opened it up. He scanned the paper.

"Why does this address sound so familia-"

He paused.

"Wait...that's," he gave a loud sigh.

"Yeesh! Not this again!" He cried angrily.

Maru opened the door.

"What's wrong...?" She asked, wiping her eyes.

"Ah...Maru," Chris looked at her.

"Want to take a ride...?"

33 Past

"Weird choice for a location..." Rick mumbled, stepping out of the cab.

He looked up at the building.

He then realized the location was part of what used to be the Labs. The building was mostly destroyed, with a lot of rubble around.

Rick closed his eyes for a moment.

He thought about the day he rescued Maru.

His thoughts then wandered on to think about the last time he saw Norio.

*

Fourteen years ago, a family was getting ready for bed. A man tucked two boys into bed.

"I'm going to go say goodnight to your sister now," the man paused for a minute.

He then gave a smile.

"Boys...I just wanted to tell you..." He gulped and looked down.

Before he could get a word out, they heard banging on the door.

The man quickly turned his attention toward the doorway.

"...Hold on." He said.

As he stepped out into the kitchen, he saw his partner standing, looking at the door.

"Larkin?" The man called out.

"Is somebody there...?"

Larkin did not answer.

"Must've been the win-" before he could finish, a few men came bursting into the house.

The man gasped.

Larkin took a step back. No emotion on his face.

"What the hell is going on!?" The man cried.

The men pushed into him, knocking him down.

The intruders ran into the bedroom where the boys were.

The younger brother screamed.

However, the older brother stood in front of him in what seemed to be an attempt to protect his younger brother—anger in his eyes.

The intruders hovered over the children, smirking.

The younger boy began trembling behind his brother.

"Grab them!" One intruder barked.

The man pinned to the ground began screaming.

"Please, what the hell is going on!?" He cried out.

"Boys!?" His voice sounded desperate.

The intruders, with the boys in their arms, smirked.

One stepped on the man's face, causing him to scream out in pain.

"Where are you taking them!?" He cried.

"Where the hell are you taking them!?" He continued shrieking.

"Larkin, do something!" He cried.

The intruder then stepped off him, walking out with the others.

The man struggled to get up.

"Mikael," Larkin looked steadily down as Mikael got up.

Mikael glared at him, panting.

"What did you do?" He glared.

Larkin didn't answer.

"Larkin, what the fuck did you do!?" He shrieked.

"Our job, no, my job here is done," Larkin said, as he smiled.

Mikael's eyes widened.

"You son of a bi-"

Larkin began walking toward the door.

"Don't you,"

He kept walking.

"Don't you dare!" Mikael screamed.

Larkin paused in the doorway.

"The older boy has some use," he said to an intruder that had stayed behind.

Mikael's vision started fading.

"The youngest," Larkin paused.

Before he heard the rest of what Larkin had to say, he fell to the floor, unconscious.

*

The younger boy struggled desperately.

"Let us go!" He shrieked.

The older boy was silent. The intruders stopped walking.

"Take him toward the facility," the intruder who had stayed behind ordered, pointing at the older brother.

The boy said nothing.

"Got it," the man carrying him said.

The intruder carrying the older boy looked at, the younger brother.

"What about him?"

The head of the intruders glared.

"Go." He ordered.

"Rick!" The younger brother cried out.

"Let him go!" He sobbed wildly.

Rick turned his head and smirked.

"Don't be such a cry baby, will you?"

The younger brothers' eyes widened.

Before he could say anything else, the man carrying him smacked him hard on the head.

"No more talking!" He barked.

Rick turned his head. However, the other men were already walking in the opposite direction.

All he saw was the bewilderment in his younger brother's eyes.

*

The men carrying the younger boy threw him to the ground.

The boy grunted.

"You know the orders," the man began.

"Kill him."

One man pulled a match out of his pocket.

Another man handed him a branch.

"That bastard, Larkin, didn't give us anything."

The boy's eyes widened at the mention of one of his father figures.

The boy sat on the ground, looking exhausted.

"Norio," a man said, lighting the branch on fire.

"This might hurt."

The man smirked, throwing the lit-on fire branch at the boy.

Norio began screaming in agony.

"No point in staying." The head said as he signaled them to leave.

Norio rolled around, desperately screaming in pain.

*

As the fire went out, Norio rolled onto his back.

Burn marks covered the right side of his body, as well as that side of his face.

Norio opened his eyes slowly.

His eyes lost their color. The color in place became despair.

He watched as a branch from the tree next to him came plummeting down.

Stabbing out his right eye.

*

By the time Norio regained consciousness, he was being carried.

"Is his eye really gone, mommy!?" A little girl cried.

A woman carrying him did not respond. She, followed by two little girls, ran desperately toward their house deep in the woods.

The world faded to black as he fell unconscious once more.

*

Rick frowned.

"I should have never said those words..."

As he looked up, Rick noticed a man standing in the rubble. His back turned.

His eyes widened.

"Norio..." he whispered to himself.

Norio looked over, noticing him.

"Happy birthday, big brother." He smirked.

34 Birthday

Rick stared for a good second.

As he stepped over some rubble, his mind went blank. However, his body kept moving.

Walking towards the boy, he let down fourteen years ago.

He opened his mouth.

"N-" He tried to get it out, but it got caught in his throat.

"Oh?" Norio turned around.

Rick quickly turned.

Chris and Maru pulled up.

"Hey!" Chris ran out.

"Wait, what the hell are you two-"

Norio stared at Maru.

"Ah." He said.

Rick quickly turned back to Norio.

"I'm sorry, I don't know why they're here-"

Norio closed his eye, nodding his head.

"Nah, it's fine." He opened his eye.

"What's the kid's name?" He questioned.

"M-"

Norio narrowed his eye at Rick.

"Let her answer." He said.

Maru looked at Chris.

"Go on," Chris said.

Rick chuckled nervously.

"M-Maru..." Maru whispered.

"Maru, huh?" Norio closed his eye, nodding.

"Maru," he opened his eye, pausing for a moment.

He then gave Rick a look.

"What would you do if I told you," Norio then paused, shaking his head.

"No, that's wrong of me."

He turned to Rick.

"Do you want to tell her what you've been up to during these past fourteen years?"

Rick's heart dropped.

He opened, then quickly shut his mouth.

"Tch," Norio sighed.

"Got cold feet, eh, Mr. Reaper...?"

Chris' eyes widened.

Rick stood there, frozen.

Maru quickly looked up.

"Does that name ring a bell...?" Norio asked.

Maru's eyes widened.

"H-hey!" Chris cried.

"Just what the hell are you trying to accomplish-"

Norio glared.

"I wouldn't get so high and mighty as the person who wiped her memories."

He closed his eye.

"Ah...guess I've said too much." He muttered.

Rick stared blankly.

Chris was speechless.

Maru looked around frantically, with fear in her eyes.

"Tch," Norio ran his fingers through his hair and huffed.

"You know...I used to look up to you." He looked down.

"What for, I wonder?" He questioned, stepping off a piece of rubble.

"Happy birthday, Rick." He muttered, looking down as he walked away.

Suddenly, Rick began laughing.

Chris quickly looked up.

Rick placed a hand on his stomach as he continued to laugh hysterically.

Chris stood there, stunned.

"Maru!" He cried out between laughs.

Maru just stood there.

He walked over, extending out his arms.

Maru slowly lifted her head.

Her eyes widened.

"Maru..." his voice broke.

He slowly knelt to the ground, wrapping his arms around her. He began to sob into her shoulder.

Maru began trembling. She continued standing there, frozen.

The one person that she had admired. He was now on his knees, breaking down into tears of absolute defeat.

The first adult that she had come to put her full trust in. He was also the man that had betrayed her.

He was the man who had murdered her best friend.

It was all too much.

Maru's eyes slowly closed. Her vision fading as she lost consciousness.

35 Believe

"Rick!" A voice cried out from behind the door.

Rick rose from the couch. He opened the door greeted by Sena.

"How is she?" Sena looked over to Maru, who was wrapped in a blanket.

Rick smiled sadly.

"I guess she could be better."

Sena looked around the room.

"How's Chris...?"

Rick frowned.

"I don't know; why don't you ask him?"

Sena sighed.

"Because he won't answer mine or Abbey's calls."

Rick scratched his head and let out a sigh.

"I'm sorry for such a short stay, but I have to go back downstairs to make sure there aren't any customers who come by."

As she stepped outside the door, they heard a whine.

Sena and Rick quickly turned around.

"Sena..." Maru whimpered.

Sena quickly went over.

"What is it, Maru...?" She said, pulling the blanket off the girl's head, stroking her hair.

"Please..." Maru began.

"Don't leave..."

Sena caressed her face.

"I'm sorry, Maru," she smiled.

"But I have to do my job."

Maru's lip quivered.

"Bye-bye," Sena said as she waved to Maru.

As she passed Rick, who was leaning near the door, she stopped.

"I may not know you as The Reaper," she paused and looked at him.

"However, I know you as the Rick whom we all believe in," she looked down, smiling sadly.

"And that includes Maru." Rick's eyes widened.

"Please, take care of yourselves." She said, walking out the door.

Rick stood there for a moment, and then he chuckled.

"That so?" He whispered to himself.

36 Fever Dream

As the day progressed, Maru remained huddled in her blanket.

"Maru," Rick gently called out.

She did not look up.

"How about we eat something?" He suggested as he began walking over.

Maru quickly hid her face in the blanket.

Rick sighed as he sat down.

"Maru, you really do need to eat something," he paused.

The blanket began shaking.

"Maru," he whispered.

"Please tell me you're not..."

He quickly pried the blanket off her head.

Maru squeaked.

Rick touched his lips to her forehead.

His eyes widened.

"You're burning up!" He cried.

He quickly rose, rushing to the refrigerator.

He went into the freezer, quickly grabbing an ice pack.

Damnit! How the hell was I so clueless!? He thought to himself.

As Rick got back to the couch, he gently placed the ice pack on the girl's forehead. She flinched.

"Maru..." He whispered, caressing her cheek.

Maru whimpered.

He sighed.

"I-" He looked down at her.

Was this really the time to tell her everything? Why he killed her best friend? She had the right to know, but was this the best opportunity?

"When you feel better..." He closed his eyes.

"We'll talk."

*

Sena walked into the apartment.

"I have medicine." She said, handing a bag to Rick.

"Sena...thank you." He said, taking the medication out.

"I don't know how I didn't notice..." She looked down.

"Relax, don't beat yourself up over it; we caught it."

Sena nodded.

"Ok, Maru," Rick said, grabbing a spoon from a drawer.

"Sena brought you medicine; you have to take it to feel better, 'kay?" He smiled.

He sat down and proceeded to pour some medication on the spoon.

"Say Aah,"

Maru looked at him.

As she slowly opened her mouth, Rick put the spoonful of medication in her mouth.

She swallowed, making a face.

Sena and Rick clapped.

"Good girl!" Rick beamed, patting her head.

Maru looked at him as if she wanted to say something.

*

As night came, Rick shut the lights in the living room.

"I'd have you come lay with me," he chuckled.

"But I don't want to get sick too..." He rubbed his head, sheepishly.

"Here," he walked over to the couch.

"Why don't you lay down."

He grabbed one of her stuffed animals.

"Mr. Bunny wants you to feel better soon!" He joked, pretending that Mr. Bunny kissed her.

Rick chuckled, amused for a second.

"Okay," he said.

"I'll be in my room."

He paused.

"I..." He knelt.

Maru weakly turned to him.

He blushed and exhaled.

"I love you, Maru..."

Maru's eyes widened.

He touched his lips to her forehead again.

"Seems like your fevers gone down..." He rose.

"Goodnight." He waved, shutting his door over a bit.

Maru stared at the door for a few moments, then turned to lay on her back.

She stared at the ceiling for a bit until she drifted off to sleep.

*

"Hey!" A voice cried out.

Maru looked around frantically. She knew that voice.

"Maru, over here!" Her eyes widened.

Stepping out from what seemed to be a fog was Cole.

He grinned.

Maru wanted to run over. However, her legs would not budge.

She could not believe it. She had not seen her best friend in months.

That's when she realized. She hadn't seen him because he was dead.

Cole frowned.

"Oh!" He closed his eyes, nodding.

"I guess you just realized, huh...?" He opened his eyes.

"That's ok!" He gave a smile.

"I..." He paused.

"I just wanted to explain everything." He looked at her.

"My best friend deserves an answer!" He giggled.

"Before I explain..."

He blushed.

"I really like your new hair!" He said, looking down sheepishly.

"A-and..." tears welled in his eyes.

"You got taller...!" He smiled.

"Oh yeah...I forgot." He giggled.

"You can't talk..." He then looked around.

"I called you here because..."

Maru looked at him.

"Well," he began.

"Rick and I..." He smiled sadly.

"We made a promise!"

Maru's eyes widened.

"I'm sorry...I know you have so many questions." He chuckled.

"Well," he began.

"Rick was sent to be my doctor." He looked at Maru to make sure she was following along.

"I know it's hard to hear, but Rick was a killer before he met us."

Cole looked down for a second.

"But, he's always had a soft spot for kids..." He said.

"Anyway, the moment he became Rick..." he closed his eyes.

"Was when he took off that mask...for the final time." He looked at her.

"That was when he was about to...kill me." He chuckled nervously.

"Maru," he began.

"The Reaper has killed...many people." He looked down.

"But,"

He looked Maru dead in the eyes.

"Rick has killed The Reaper."

Maru swallowed.

Cole then smiled.

"It's about time he finally told you, huh..." He chuckled.

"I'm glad he finally told you he loves you!" He beamed.

"I have to go..." He quickly said.

"Please, Maru," he began.

"One!" He shouted.

"Never forget those three words; it's not easy for him!" He looked at the giant clock on the wall.

"Two!" He continued.

"Tell him everything!" The clock was about to strike the next minute.

"Three!" He paused.

"Please...forgive him."

The room went white.

Maru caught a glimpse of Cole mouthing three words.

*

As she awoke, Maru gasped for air.

She quickly sat up on the couch.

She touched her face, breathing heavily.

"Rick!" She cried, running into his room.

Rick sprang up quickly.

"W-What!?" He cried out, half asleep.

Maru jumped on the bed, crawling on top of him.

"I know everything!" She cried.

Rick looked at her.

"W-What do you mean...?" He asked, stroking her hair.

"Cole told me...!"

Rick's eyes widened.

"You have to believe me!" She looked at him.

Rick slowly raised his hand to Maru's forehead.

Her fever was gone.

"I believe you..." He whispered, stunned.

Maru began tearing up.

"I'm glad..." she whispered.

"I'm glad you're Rick!"

Rick's eyes welled up.

"C-come here..." He said, holding out his arms.

The two embraced.

Maru began sobbing into him.

Rick teary-eyed, stroked her hair.

*

A few minutes later, Maru was fast asleep in Rick's arms.

Rick stared at the ceiling.

"Cole..." he whispered.

"Thank you..." he smiled.

Closing his eyes, he drifted off to sleep.

37 Night Life

The city was bustling as night fell.

In the middle of the commotion was a bar.

The bar was quite empty in contrast to the outside bustle. However, business went on.

As the door creaked open, leaking a hint of the night into the dim-lit bar, a cloaked man entered.

"Ah, welcome." The bartender greeted.

The man simply gave a wave.

Only one other customer was seated at the bar.

"What can I get for you?" The bartender asked the man.

"I don't care." The man replied.

The bartender looked at him for a second.

"Uh," he began.

"D-do you have an ID...?"

The man blushed.

"H-here..." He grumbled, pulling out his ID.

The other man seated at the bar looked as if he had caught a glimpse; his eyes widened.

The bartender gave a nod.

The man sat next to the other bar visitor.

The other man kept his gaze on his glass.

"Nice night," the cloaked man said.

The man next to him gave a slight nod in reply.

*

As the night progressed, and after only a couple of drinks, the cloaked man was nearly asleep at the counter.

The other man downed one last glass.

He paused.

Studying the cloaked man for a moment, he gave a sad smile.

The man proceeded to take off his coat, laying it on top of the passed-out cloaked man.

He gave one final glance before leaving the bar.

I'm glad to see you're alive, Mikael. He thought to himself as he walked off into the night.

38 Fallen Angel

By the time Larkin arrived back, he had figured everyone would be fast asleep.

But as he opened the door, he was greeted by a familiar pink presence.

"Papa!" She cried, throwing her arms around him.

Larkin, completely caught off guard, patted her head awkwardly.

"Kari..." He began.

"Shouldn't you...be in bed?"

She sniffled, looking up.

"Mim said we had something to discuss!" She grabbed his hand.

"We're in the meeting room, papa!"

As she led him to the room, Larkin couldn't help but think about those kids. The kids he betrayed so many years ago.

It was merely a game of pretending... He thought to himself.

As the two came up to their meeting room, the door opened to reveal two other people sitting at a business table.

"Yo," A man with pink hair gave a wave.

"Any news?"

The other person, a lady, stood up.

"One of our spies found two possible candidates. She said, tapping a pointer to the projector screen.

"Those are..." Larkin frowned.

"Those are children, Janine." He sighed.

Janine grinned.

"They are children...but they're Lab children."

Larkin looked up quickly.

"Any files you were able to hack?"

Janine gave a nod. She pointed to the girl on the right.

"This is 247," Janine began.

"Her powers harvested only in her right arm."

Larkin frowned.

"Then what's the p-"

Janine closed her eyes and smiled.

She then pointed to the girl on the left.

"This one is 246," she began.

"Her power transferred to both of her arms, making her insanely strong."

Larkin nodded.

"So, what is the plan, Ms. strategist...?"

Janine grinned.

"Why, we use both of these children and transfer their powers to you...boss."

Larkin grinned.

"Excellent."

Kari, who was standing in the hallway, listening in, listened in complete confusion.

"Now," Larkin paused.

"What are our plans to obtain them?"

Mim pointed to himself proudly.

"I've got you, boss."

Larkin turned to Mim.

"How so?"

Mim smirked.

"I'll use my precise imitation skills, pretending to be their guardians, and lure them out."

Larkin nodded.

"Excellent now..." He paused.

"What do we do in case there are intruders?"

Mim gave Janine a nervous glance.

Janine laughed nervously.

"That's the...only flaw in our plan, actually."

Larkin frowned.

"What do you mean?"

Mim rubbed his head.

"Well, when I watched the Takeshi family circus."

Larkin's eyes widened.

"They seemed pretty flexible," Mim chuckled.

"Did you s-"

Mim turned to Janine, not hearing Larkin.

"As for 246's family..." She bit her lip.

"Well...her guardian is..." She laughed nervously.

"He's an infamous killer known as The Reaper..."

Larkin froze.

"We'll be able to power through 'em, though!" Mim cried.

"We'll have both kids by the time they even try shit!" He exclaimed.

Larkin looked at them for a minute.

"Fine, we'll go with this plan." He said, turning to walk out.

"Heading to bed, boss?" Mim asked.

Larkin nodded as he walked out.

Janine turned to Mim, who, in return, shrugged.

*

As Larkin walked down the corridors, he noticed Kari's door was open.

As he poked his head in, he noticed her sitting on the edge of her bed, looking out a window.

"I don't know what's best..."

He froze as she began.

"I don't want to hurt innocent people, but!" She smiled sadly.

"I owe papa for everything he's done for me..."

Larkin cleared his throat.

Kari quickly turned around.

"P-papa...!" She exclaimed, running up to the doorway.

"Papa I..."

Larkin's cold stare broke into a smile quickly.

"Kari..." He began as he gently placed a hand on her head.

"You should go to bed." He smiled softly.

She looked at him for a minute.

"Y-yes...!" She cried.

"G'night, papa!" She cried as she ran to her bed.

"Goodnight, Kari." He said, shutting her bedroom door.

*

Kari looked out the window as she laid in her bed.

"Did he...hear my prayers?" She paused.

"Is he really an angel that saved me, or..." She shut her eyes.

"He's a fallen angel..." She whispered, smiling sadly as she drifted off to sleep.

39 Kidnapped

"Hey," Keren began, placing her hands on her hips.

Norio looked up from the newspaper.

"Hah?"

Keren frowned.

"You've been even more irritatingly quiet lately."

Norio looked back down at the paper.

"Oi! Don't go ignoring me, you jerk!" Keren cried.

Norio groaned.

"It's too early for your crap!" He grumbled as he got up.

Keren folded her arms and sighed.

*

As he got breakfast ready, Norio turned to Emersyn and Vera.

"Do you two want to help put the blueberries in?"

The two quickly looked up.

"Really!?" Emersyn cried.

"Mm!" Vera nodded eagerly.

It's not that big a deal... Norio thought to himself.

Keren leaning on the wall, gave a smile.

"He's really at his best when it comes to these kids..."
She whispered, smiling.

*

As the day progressed, it proved to be a lazy kind of
day. Everyone was lying around the house, bored.

Keren let out a loud groan.

"You guys are boring me to absolute death!" She
cried, getting up.

"Where are you going?" Vera asked.

"Somewhere with a sign of life!" She huffed, walking
out the door.

Emersyn, sitting on Norio's lap, looked up at him.

Norio, who was busy reading a book, looked at her.

"Yeah?" He asked.

"I love you!" Emersyn said, beaming.

Norio blushed and quickly looked at the floor.

Vera looked up from her book and smiled.

Norio quickly went back to reading his book.

Emersyn frowned.

Norio looked at her again.

"Now, what is it?" Norio asked.

Emersyn puffed her cheeks in frustration.

"Dummy!" She cried out.

Norio looked at her, shocked.

 As she stormed out of the room, Norio looked at Vera, who, in turn, pretended not to notice.

He let out a sigh.

*

As night came, Keren was still out, Norio had gone on a walk, and Vera was next door with Norio's sisters.

 Emersyn sat up on the couch, hugging a pillow.

"Dummy..." she sniffled.

"Oi," A voice called out.

Emersyn looked around, confused. She then realized it was Norio's voice.

She couldn't see him, however.

She folded her arms.

"I'm not talking to you!" She exclaimed.

"Just open the garage door; I'm sorry."

Emersyn's eyes widened.

"R-really...?" She asked.

"Yes, really." His tone sounded soft and sincere.

"F-fine...!" Emersyn said, walking to press the button on the garage.

"Nori..." she paused.

"Huh?"

She frowned.

"I'm too short..." She said pouting.

He sighed.

"Grab a stool with that strength of yours."

Emersyn frowned.

"Fine!" She grumbled, grabbing the stool single-handedly with her bandaged arm.

As she climbed the stool, she pressed the button.

"Good girl..."

As the garage opened, however, it wasn't Norio waiting on the other side.

A man draped in a cloak smirked.

Emersyn's eyes widened.

"Y-you're not..." Before she could finish, she fell unconscious.

The cloaked man caught her, letting out a laugh.

"Man, too easy..." He snickered as he ran off into the woods.

40 Leader

As Keren walked up to the steps, she was shocked to see Norio standing on the porch.

As he lifted his head, a despair filled his eye.

"What the hell happened!?" She exclaimed, running up to him.

"Somebody took her," Norio replied.

"What do you mean!?" Keren cried.

"Come," he said, grabbing her by the wrist.

As they walked to the back, the garage door was left open.

"No..." Keren covered her mouth.

"I just went on a walk," he paused.

"By the time I got back..." He looked down.

"She wasn't happy with me but,"

Keren shot him a look.

"What do you mean...?"

Norio sighed.

"She told me she...loved me."

Keren looked at him.

"Are you sure this is a case of kidnapping and not,"

Norio shot her a look.

"I'm damn sure, Emersyn wouldn't get so upset she'd leave because of three words."

Keren let out a sigh.

"Where is Vera?"

Norio pointed to his sister's house.

"She was over there during all of this."

Keren looked at him.

"Does she know?"

Norio nodded.

"We need to do something."

Norio folded his arms.

"Any ideas?"

Keren nodded.

"Missing children posters, we can go into town."

Norio looked at her, then gave a nod.

"We'll go tomorrow." He said.

"What!? Why tomorrow!?" She cried, stomping her foot.

"Because it might not be safe."

Keren looked down.

"Right..." She whispered.

*

As he got in bed, Norio looked up at the ceiling.

"Please...let her be safe." He sighed, laying down.

*

The next day, the two went right to work.

They began plastering wanted posters on every possible surface.

Sena was finishing up with a customer; as she waved goodbye, she looked out the window, noticing a poster. She quickly ran outside.

"Excuse me,"

Keren looked up quickly.

"Oh..." Keren looked down.

"We really need to hang these everywhere we can."

Sena shook her head.

"That's not an issue," she paused.

"I just think you might need help is all..." Sena said, giving a smile.

Keren looked at her, then smiled.

"Thanks..." Keren said, handing her a pile of posters.

As the two went around, Keren spotted Norio.

"Oi!" She shouted.

As Sena looked up, she froze.

"Nothing,"

Norio looked at Sena.

"You're..."

Keren looked back and forth quickly.

"Oh her?" She asked.

"She just wanted to help."

Sena gave a nod.

Norio turned.

"I see." He said, clearing his throat.

"Is there some kind of tension I'm missing here...?" Keren asked.

Norio shot her a look.

"None that concerns you."

Keren smirked.

"Nori..." She grinned.

"You didn't tell me you had a lover!" She giggled.

"She's not my ex!" He cried.

"Oi, Sena, say something!"

Sena looked at them flustered.

"I'm...his brothers' friend."

Norio looked down.

"He's not my brother..."

Keren gave a nod.

"I get the picture now..." She said, smiling sadly.

"Anyways, thanks for your help, Sena," Norio said, taking the posters.

"We got it from here." He said.

Sena gave a nod.

"Good luck..." she whispered, walking away.

"Nori," Keren began.

Before she could finish, the two heard their phones ding.

"Weird, we both got texts at the same time; what are the odds of," she froze as her eyes widened as she read the text.

*

As Sena arrived back at her place, she noticed Chris had his car parked in front of her shop.

As she walked up the stairs, she knocked on the door to Rick's apartment.

Then she heard her phone ding. As her eyes skimmed the message, she froze.

"Rick!" She cried, banging on the door.

The door quickly swung open.

"Chris!" She exclaimed.

"Come in!" He said.

As she stepped in, he quickly began shutting and locking the door.

Rick, who was seated on the couch, looked up.

"You're safe..." He whispered.

Chris looked at his watch.

"Looks like everyone's here." He said.

The room was silent for what felt like forever.

"So," Rick began, breaking the silence.

"We all got that text," he said.

"Did everyone get the same text?"

Tammy looked up.

"What does yours say...?" She asked.

Rick clicked open his messages.

"Tomorrow, go to the abandoned dojo on Grove Lane, (fear not, there's a key to get in). If you do not comply, I have no choice but to harm your loved one(s). PS, bring the kid, or else." Rick looked steadily down.

"Man..." Chris began.

Abbey looked up.

"That's my father's dojo..." She whispered.

Chris folded his arms.

"Looks like whoever's behind this knows about us and our personal business."

He turned to Rick.

"You're good at strategy," he began.

"What do you suggest we do...?"

Everyone quickly turned their attention to Rick.

"The fact that this person knows enough about us and how we're all connected," he looked up.

"This is undoubtedly a serious threat." He sighed.

"The text was so vague, though," Tammy said, looking up.

"What if there's a threat waiting for us when we get there...?"

Chris smirked.

"Oi," Abbey glared.

"What's so funny, curly?"

Chris chuckled.

"Did you all forget about our trump card?" He then turned, pointing at Rick.

"As long as we have him..."

Everyone in the room turned to look at Rick.

"You ready, leader?" Chris asked.

Everyone smiled.

"Ah." Rick smiled, closing his eyes, leaning back on the couch.

"I'm always ready."

41 My Promise to You

As the next day came, everyone arrived outside of Sena's shop.

"Where's Rick?" Tammy asked.

"He's still getting ready," Chris answered.

"How'd you guys sleep?" Chris asked as he looked around.

"Not really well..." Sena replied as Abbey let out a yawn.

They then heard the creaking of the outside steps.

"What the hell took you so long?" Chris asked.

"Sorry, sorry," Rick said, scratching his head.

"Maru," Tammy began.

"How are you?"

Maru, who was half asleep, rubbed her eyes.

"I'm really sleepy..."

Tammy giggled.

As they began walking toward the dojo, Abbey momentarily stopped.

"So, what's the game plan, leader?" Abbey asked.

"We go in with our guards up is all," Rick said.

"What the hell kind of vague plan is," Before she could finish, Rick, carrying a sleepy Maru, looked over his shoulder at her.

"One of you will stand outside with Maru, in

 case." Abbey frowned.

"But still..." She mumbled.

"Maybe Tammy should," Sena said.

Tammy looked up.

"Eh...?"

Chris nodded his head.

"You're the second youngest here, plus you're not,"

He quickly shut his mouth.

Tammy looked at him.

"Not what Chris...?" She asked.

"I think what they're trying to get at is that you're not physically on par with the rest of us," Rick said.

"I guess..." Tammy frowned.

"Besides, we'll be inside if there's commotion out there; we'll hear it." Rick smiled.

Tammy nodded.

*

"Well, here we are," Chris announced.

Abbey stared for a moment.

"Abbey..." Sena said, reaching for her hand.

Abbey blushed.

"I'm good, really, Sena." She smiled, taking her hand.

"Hold up," Rick said as he handed a sleeping Maru to Chris.

"What's up...?" Chris asked cautiously.

"It's...unlocked."

Tammy quickly opened the text.

"The threat said there'd be a key, though..."

Before anyone could say anything, the door began to open. Everyone quickly got on guard.

As the door opened, it revealed Keren.

"You guys too..." Keren whispered.

Norio, seated in a chair, looked over, his eye widened.

*

"Here, this is the letter..." Keren said, placing it down in the middle of the table.

Rick grabbed it, quickly skimming through it.

Norio kept his head turned away.

"Well?" Abbey said.

"Read it out loud," Tammy whispered.

"It says," Rick began.

"Glad to know you've all made it. By now, I am sure you've learned there's no serious threat, yet. However, the true danger will be found at the location listed on the back. Please stay on guard; your life depends on it. I left a few weapons around the building as well, thank you, Abbey."

Rick then flipped it over.

"This is..." Rick looked at Chris.

"Isn't this another part of the labs?" He asked.

Chris leaned in to look.

"Yup, that's a secluded, abandoned part of the labs." He paused.

"It's somewhere near Ocleau Forest."

Keren looked up.

"But we live in the forest...how have we never seen it...?"

Norio scoffed.

"The forest is big, dummy."

Keren puffed her cheeks in annoyance.

Chris stared at the paper, then sighed.

"This really isn't a joke..." He muttered.

The room fell silent.

"What are the weapons...?" Tammy asked, breaking the silence.

"Three swords," Abbey said as she knelt to pick them up.

"Only three...?" Keren asked.

"When there's...seven adults."

She turned to Norio.

"Did I count that right?"

Norio nodded his head.

"Who here knows how to fight using a sword?" Chris asked.

Sena and Abbey raised their hands. Chris turned to Rick.

"Raise your hand."

Rick grumbled, raising his hand.

"Oh...that's only three of us," Tammy said, scanning the room.

"Are you three really ok with that...?"

They turned to her.

"Using the sword would mean you'd potentially be killing..."

Sena looked at Abbey, concerned.

"Listen," Abbey began.

"They're threatening our lives; it's all in self-defense." She crossed her arms and let out a sigh.

"I have no qualms..." She turned to Sena.

"You ok...?" She asked.

Sena nodded.

"You're right...I just."

She looked down.

"I'll just try my best to avoid using it unless I need to, I guess..."

Abbey smiled sadly, taking her hand.

"If you don't want to, I understand..." she said, stroking her hand.

"If that's the case... I'll be your shield, just until you can unsheathe."

Sena looked up at her.

"Abbey..." she whispered.

Rick turned to look at Maru, who was asleep in the corner of the room.

"I'm fine with whatever." Chris chuckled.

Rick turned to Norio.

"Anyways...why are you here?"

Norio closed his eye.

"They have my kid."

Keren nodded.

"They kidnapped Emersyn a couple of nights ago..."

Rick's eyes widened.

"That doesn't make sense...why would they take your kid and not..."

Norio frowned.

"Maybe they didn't see the opportunity, and that's why we're all here."

Chris looked around.

"Someone knows what's up over there..." He grumbled.

"Maybe the threat is giving us a chance..." He sighed.

"Are you saying the threat might be on our side?" Tammy asked.

Norio looked up.

"Or this is all some sick joke to lure us in." He closed his eye.

"I refuse to kill," he began.

"I actually took lessons in hand-to-hand combat some years ago." He continued.

Rick looked at him and gave a nod.

"Well, whatever's waiting for us over there," he began.

"I think we're ready to face whatever may come."

He glanced over at Maru.

"I really don't want her to be exposed to all of this..." He sighed.

"She's been through enough at her age."

The room fell silent once more.

"How about a blindfold...?" Tammy suggested.

Rick looked at her.

"Someone will just have to carry her, I guess." She said.

Rick gave a nod.

"I'll go home and get mine."

As everyone stood up to leave, Rick paused.

"Listen," he began.

"I put my trust in every one of you...I won't let anyone of you die," he paused.

"That's my promise to all of you."

Everyone smiled.

"Yeesh, do you have a promise kink or something...?" Chris said, laughing.

Rick chuckled.

"Just shut up, and don't die...I'm counting on you."

Chris nodded. "Ah, I'll do whatever it takes to make your promises come true."

Chris watched as Rick left.

He let out a sigh.

Abbey gave him a playful punch. "Let's go, Romeo; we don't have all day to flirt."

Chris chuckled.

"Funny coming from you."

Abbey blushed.

"S-shut up..." She grumbled.

"It's just...I'll do anything to see the man who gave my life a purpose happy," Chris said, closing his eyes and smiling.

42 Entrance

"Nori..." Keren whispered.

"Hah?" He said in response, looking down at his phone.

"Are we almost there yet?"

Norio frowned.

"Do you want Emersyn back or not?"

Keren shot him a look.

"Don't be silly!" She cried.

"Shh!" Rick put a finger to his mouth.

"We could have driven, but then they'd definitely see us coming," Chris said, sighing.

*

"Boss," Mim began, walking into the room.

"Hm?" Larkin turned around.

"One of our spies claimed to have sent out threats."

Larkin nodded.

"This just got very interesting," Larkin said with a grin.

*

"Hold on!" Tammy cried out.

Everyone turned to look at her.

"My phone lost its signal..." She whispered.

"What do you expect? We're in the middle of a forest." Norio sighed.

"Looks like we're," before he could finish, Chris suddenly pointed.

"Behind those trees..." He whispered.

"Is that it...?" Sena questioned.

"Rick..." Maru whispered.

"Don't worry, I have you," Rick reassured her.

"Just keep that blindfold on no matter what, okay?"

Maru nodded.

*

"So, they've made it..." A cloaked figure said, watching from a balcony.

The cloaked figure smiled as it walked away.

*

Rick peeked his head from behind a bush.

"There are two guards..." He whispered.

He quickly scanned the group.

"Someone watch Maru," he then paused.

"Norio, come with me."

Norio quickly looked up.

"Relax, I know you don't want to kill them." He said, then smirked.

"Just make a cool entrance with me is all."

Norio slowly rose.

"Be careful..." Abbey whispered.

*

Everyone held their breath as the two of them snuck around behind plants, and trees, getting closer to the entrance.

"Do you hear something...?" One of the guards asked.

"Must be the wind..."

Suddenly, a sword came flying at one of the guard's chests, impaling him.

"Who goes there!?" The other guard cried out.

"Sorry, sorry," Rick said from behind a tree.

"The wind was so strong; my sword slipped into your buddy there."

The guard's eyes widened.

"Show yourself!" He shrieked.

Suddenly, a quick punch came at him, knocking him unconscious.

Norio sighed as he blew on his knuckle.

Rick, grabbing the sword, grinned. The two stood back to back.

"How's that for an entrance?" Norio said, smirking.

43 Surprise

"Now!" Rick cried out.

More enemies came pouring out of the entrance.

The rest of the group came charging out from behind the bushes.

Rick cut through a few of the enemies with ease.

"Sena!" Abbey cried as she drew her sword, running in front of her.

"I knew you'd be reluctant!" She cried.

"But!" Sena yelled.

"I need to be of use somehow!" She shouted.

"If you want to be of use," Keren began.

"Shut that pretty mouth of yours and throw punches!" She cried.

Sena gave a determined nod.

"Chris!" Rick shouted.

"Hey!" He replied.

"How are you holding up with Maru!?" He cried out.

Maru, clinging to Chris's shoulder, whimpered.

"Fine!" He said as he kicked an enemy.

The enemy quickly got back up.

"Tch!" Chris grumbled, kicking him again.

"Stay down, you damn cockroach!" He shouted.

One of the enemies from behind him began chuckling. Chris quickly turned.

"Your kicks are weak...funny how you think you'll be able to protect that girl-"

Chris quickly kicked him in the mouth, knocking him down.

"Shut the hell up!" He cried.

"Chris..." Tammy whispered as she dodged an enemy.

"The hell are there so many of them for!?" Keren cried out.

"A door!" Tammy shouted.

Rick quickly ran up from behind her, cutting down enemies.

"Damnit, watch your back, Tammy!" He yelled.

"S-sorry!" Tammy stammered, examining the door.

"Where's the handle..." She whispered.

Rick quickly slammed into the door, blocking it from an incoming enemy.

"It's some sort of weird metal..."

Norio ran up to them, pressing a button next to it. The door opened.

"Everybody inside!" Rick shouted.

As Chris ran towards the door, an enemy grabbed him by the ankle.

"Let go!" He cried, stomping on his hand.

The enemy let out a cry.

"Tch..." He then looked at Maru.

"I've got you, shrimp..." He said as he stroked her hair.

Maru whimpered in response.

*

As everyone made it into the room, Norio quickly pressed a button to shut the door.

"We all made it..." He sighed in relief.

"Round one, complete." Rick chuckled.

"This is a weird setup, though..." Tammy pointed out.

"Eh?" Rick said as they turned to her.

"Why would there be food here..."

Suddenly, there was clapping.

Everyone quickly turned around.

Stepping out of the shadows, a man continued clapping. Behind him was a young woman.

"A good observation, Tammy." He smiled.

Abbey quickly drew her sword.

"Why, you bastard..."

The man simply chuckled.

"What's the matter, Rick, Norio...?" He smiled.

"You two look like you've just seen a ghost."

Everyone quickly turned to the two, who were frozen.

"M-M..." Norio's lip quivered.

"You're Mikael..." Rick whispered.

Mikael began walking over. He placed a hand on each of the boy's shoulders.

"Save it for later..." The woman said, keeping an icy stare.

"Wait for a second..." Rick said, looking at her.

"Iris Azalea..."

Mikael chuckled nervously.

"Sorry, your sister's right..." He said, getting up.

"Hey..." Chris whispered.

"Yes, Chris?" Mikael turned to him.

He gulped.

"If you know my name, are you...the threat?"

Mikael smiled.

"Oh?" He said.

"Is that what you've named me?" He chuckled.

Keren frowned.

"You could have just said in parenthesis who you were..." She said.

Mikael closed his eyes.

"I suppose...but that would have just sucked the fun out of it." He smiled.

"Anyway..." Mikael said.

"I promise the food's not poisonous," he began.

"Please, eat up; you'll need the strength..." He smiled.

"We'll use this as our first base; there are beds in here as well...as you can tell." He said.

"You'll have to sleep two in a bed, and two of you will have to sleep on the floor, though..." He chuckled.

"Sorry about that..." he said.

"Hold on..." Rick spoke up.

Mikael turned to him.

"What about the enemies? They could easily press the switch to get in here..."

Mikael smiled.

"Don't be silly; you've already cleared the first group of enemies successfully." He said.

"This...is being played off as a game," Chris said.

"How do we know you're not the one who planned this...?"

Iris Azalea quickly drew a knife, holding it to Chris's throat.

"Don't be dumb." She muttered.

Chris threw his hands up in a panic.

"Nah..." Rick began.

"It's not Mikael we have to worry about, but..." He looked at the floor.

"I don't like what I'm getting at..." Norio looked at him.

"You don't think..."

Rick smiled sadly.

"I wouldn't put it past him, Nori."

Norio looked down.

"Yeah..." he whispered.

"Oi!" Chris suddenly cried out.

They turned to him.

"A little help here!" He cried.

The two began chuckling.

"I.A., leave him alone." Mikael scolded.

Iris Azalea quickly withdrew the knife.

Chris sighed in relief.

*

As night came, everyone lay asleep in their beds.

Rick and Norio left on the floor.

Maru, fast asleep, laid on top of Rick.

"Hey..." Rick whispered.

"You awake...?"

Norio, staring at the ceiling, nodded.

"What would have happened if I had reached out to you that day..."

Norio kept staring at the ceiling.

"Beats me..." He whispered.

"Wasn't in your control..."

Rick, holding Maru, nodded.

"Sorry about your kid." He said.

"Don't be..." Norio kept his gaze fixed on the ceiling.

"I have a feeling we'll get her back." He whispered.

Rick smiled sadly as he closed his eyes.

44 Second Chances

"Are we ready?" Rick asked, looking around the room.

There were several nods.

"Great," he paused. "Now here's the strategy," he began, using a pointer on a projector.

"We're going to split up."

Whispers were going around.

"Don't you think that's dangerous?" Abbey asked.

Rick shook his head.

"I think it'll get us to our goal quicker."

He pointed to the projector.

"Keren, Abbey, Sena, and Tammy, you guys will go towards the Eastern wing.

"Mikael, Iris Azalea, and I will head toward the Northern wing."

He looked at Norio and Chris.

"You two will go toward the Western wing," he paused.

"With Maru." The two of them looked at him.

"Rick, you can't be serious," Chris quickly paused as Rick narrowed his eyes.

 "No objections, right?" Mikael asked as he stood up.

"To make our lives much easier, we have these walkie-talkies we can use to keep each other up to date." He smiled.

"Now," he began.

"There are four higher-ups I should warn you all about."

Rick looked at him.

"Janine is in charge of tech; she can control weapons, rooms, and computers."

He pulled up a picture on the projector.

"Next," he began.

"Mim," he paused.

"Norio, Keren, my guess is Mim is the one who is responsible for kidnapping Emersyn." He cleared his throat.

"Anyway, Mim specializes in a picture-perfect voice mimicking; he's also insanely quick."

He clicked the image on the projector to Mim.

"Next," he started.

"We have Kari," he paused.

"Kari specializes in building bombs; she's a brilliant kid as you can imagine."

Mikael narrowed his eyes.

"However," he paused.

"Out of the four, she's the least to go out of her way to instigate, but even then, be careful."

Mikael looked at Norio and Rick, letting out a sigh.

"Lastly, we have him."

The projector moved on from Kari, over to a familiar face.

Norio's eye widened.

Rick looked on, completely stunned.

"Larkin," Mikael began, smiling sadly.

"He's in charge of all of this," he paused.

"Most likely, we won't have to worry about him until we succeed."

Mikael frowned.

"If he succeeds in harvesting Emersyn's power, he'll be insanely strong in hand-to-hand combat."

Mikael looked up.

"Boys," he began.

"For now, forget about the past," he looked at Norio.

"As much as it hurts, this man is responsible for everything that happened back then."

Iris Azalea looked over at Norio.

"Mikael, will he be ok tasked with this mission...?" She whispered.

Mikael looked up, noticing Norio slightly shaking.

"Norio." He said sternly.

"Do you want her back or not!?"

Rick grabbed his shoulder quickly. "Snap out of it, Nori!" He shouted.

Norio's eye quickly widened.

"S-sorry...I just."

Mikael narrowed his eyes.

"Rick, are we ready?"

Rick looked at him and gave a nod.

"No complaints." He then patted Norio on the shoulder.

"Hey, look at me." He said.

Norio slowly lifted his head.

"We knew that this was a possibility yesterday, right?" He asked.

Norio gave a slight nod.

"This man took my chance of life away for a long time," he paused.

"The people in this room gave me a second chance, and like hell, I'll let that bastard take my life away again." He closed his eyes.

"We'll give him back the pain he caused us...ten times harder."

Norio looked at him.

"Rick..."

Chris grabbed his other shoulder.

"C'mon, we got this!"

Norio smiled.

"Ah." He closed his eye and gave a nod.

"We'll give him everything we've got."

45 Broken

"This way," Chris whispered.

"Hold up," Norio said, stopping.

"Huh?" Chris turned.

"I'm going to check out this room; you go check the one next door."

Chris looked at him.

"Eh!?" He cried.

"Relax, I'll be right next door," Norio reassured.

"I don't get the point, but whatever..." Chris said, letting out a sigh.

*

As they stepped into the room, Chris placed Maru down.

"You ok, kiddo?" Chris asked.

"Mm," Maru replied.

"Good." He smiled.

"Why don't you take that thing off for now?" He said, bending down.

"Hey, Chris!" A voice called out from behind the door.

Chris froze.

"Rick...?" Chris whispered, standing up.

"What happened to splitting up?" He asked.

"Nothing, I changed my mind; I want to take Maru with me."

Chris narrowed his eyes.

"Open the door, would you?" The voice asked.

"...Prove it's you." He said.

"C'mon, man; I just want to see my kid."

Suddenly, the door opened.

Mim smirked.

Chris gasped.

"Hand over the kid," Mim began, taking a step forward.

"Chris..." Maru whimpered.

"Hold on shrimp; we'll get out of h-"

Before he could finish, Mim seemingly disappeared.

Chris looked around the room in confusion.

"Where'd he g-"

Suddenly, Mim came within inches of him, punching him across the face.

"Chris!" Maru shrieked.

"Yeesh, I did tell you to hand her over, didn't I?"

Chris stumbled but managed to regain his balance.

"Like hell!" He cried.

"I made a promise..." He began as he formed a fist.

"And I'll do anything to protect that promise!" He cried.

Mim frowned.

"You're not going to make this easy, are you?" Mim asked as he let out a sigh.

"Hand the runt over."

Chris glared.

"Over my dead body."

Mim narrowed his eyes.

"Hoh?" He grinned, disappearing once again.

Chris stood on alert, surveying the room.

Suddenly, Mim reappeared with a pole in his hand.

"If you won't hand her over," he said, as he readied the pole.

"I'll just have to take her by force!" He cried out, impaling Chris through the back to the chest.

Chris's eyes widened at the

blow. "Chris!" Maru shrieked.

Mim smirked, hovering over Maru.

"No need…" Mim began, closing his eyes.

"His body, spirit, as well as his promise, are already broken." He grinned as he scooped Maru up.

"See you," Mim said, winking as he left.

Chris's hand twitched. He tried lifting it to reach out. But it was too late.

He groaned as his blood pooled around him.

Sorry, Rick...I wanted to be with you until the end. I wanted to protect you, her, and our promise.

I just...wanted to be a better version of myself.
I wanted to atone...together.

As he thought this to himself, he weakly smiled.

He then rested his hand on the ground.

Tears filled his eyes.

Guess I was meant to be a good-for-nothing after all...
He thought as tears streamed down his face.

He weakly hacked up blood.

This type of death does suit me, huh...

He smiled, closing his eyes.

46 Synchronize

Footsteps quickly came running down the hall. The door slammed open, revealing Norio.

"Holy shit." He gasped, staring at Chris.

"Tch, I really didn't want to use this if I didn't need to, but," he began, as he started digging in his pants pocket.

"Oi, you better be alive, idiot." He said, kneeling.

Chris slightly twitched.

"Listen," Norio huffed.

"If you care about them, if you love my brother, you'll get the hell up and continue fighting!" Norio cried.

He then pulled out a tiny bottle labeled 'The Cure.'

"Looks like you'll need a bit more than Emersyn did..." He said, pouring a little into Chris's mouth.

He narrowed his eye.

"Swallow." He scolded.

Suddenly, Chris started coughing.

"Damnit, that tastes awful." He muttered, wiping his mouth with his sleeve.

"Now's not the time to bitch and moan," Norio said, helping him up.

"Tch, you're in no shape to fight." He shut his eye.

Norio wrapped an arm around Chris to help him stand.

"Guess it'll take a while to kick in since your injuries were near-fatal."

He narrowed his eye as he noticed Chris staring at the ground.

"Oi." He said.

Chris looked at him with tears in his eyes.

"What do I tell Rick..." He whispered.

Norio sighed as they hobbled down the corridor.

"Looks will say it all." He muttered.

Chris looked at Norio, then back at the floor.

"Don't think too hard on it, idiot." Norio scolded.

Chris nodded.

"This way," Norio said as the corridor led to a door.

"Rick said they've got most of the enemies done with."

Norio let out a sigh.

"I can't just leave you out here either, in case someone gets you." He grumbled.

"We'll try to sneak through; you ready?"

Chris gave a nod.

As the door opened, there were numerous enemy bodies on the ground.

Only a little more than a handful of enemies remained.

Rick quickly turned around.

His eyes widened as he saw the two of them.

As an enemy tried to attack him, he quickly stabbed and head-butted him as he let out a roar.

Mikael looked up.

"Where is..." He looked at Chris.

"No..." he whispered.

*

Mim walked into the main room. Larkin turned around.

"What's this...?" He said, pointing to an unconscious Maru.

"This is 246," Mim began.

"She's the girl with the power coursing through both of her arms." He grinned.

"How did you..." Larkin looked at him; then closed his eyes.

"No, perhaps that doesn't matter." He smirked.

"Put her in," he began.

"247's power synchronization is almost done..."

Mim peered into the glass, containing Emersyn.

"Wow..." he whispered in astonishment.

Larkin grinned.

"Looks like our plan is coming together quite nicely..." He chuckled.

"Excellent..." He then turned to Mim.

"Where is Janine?"

Mim looked at him.

"Don't know, probably in the control room, if I had to guess."

Larkin nodded.

"I see." He then placed a hand on Mim's shoulder.

"Go relax; your job, for now, is done."

Mim looked at him, then smiled.

"Yeesh, what a softy you are, boss." He chuckled, walking away.

Larkin walked back to the tubes containing Emersyn and now Maru. He frowned.

"Why do I feel this way..." He chuckled.

"Perhaps I am a softy..." He whispered as he walked away.

47 Kaboom

After all the enemies had been taken down, Rick panted.

"Listen," he began.

"Norio, you go find the ladies," he then turned to Chris.

"You stay here and don't move a damn muscle."

Chris, sitting up against the wall, gave a nod.

*

"This place gives me the creeps..." Tammy whispered.

"It feels like something can jump out at any given moment..."

As they turned a corner, everyone froze.

They were met with Kari.

Kari jumped back.

"O-Oi, you're..." Abbey whispered.

"Please...don't hurt us..." Kari whispered, tearing up.

"How do we know you won't attack us..." Keren questioned.

"I-I never wanted to hurt anybody..." Kari said as she sniffled.

"But your pal certainly did," Abbey said.

"Huh?" Kari quickly looked up.

"Don't play dumb; I'm sure you've been communicating this entire time," Abbey said, glaring.

"I promise I don't know anything!" Kari cried out.

Tammy narrowed her eyes.

"This will get us nowhere." She said, taking a step forward.

"Tammy...?" Sena whispered.

"Oi, don't get too close!" Abbey cried.

"If you mean everything you've said..." She said, taking a few more steps.

"Drop your weapon."

Kari's eyes widened.

She then slowly lifted the twirler off her belt and dropped it to the floor.

"Now..." Tammy looked at her.

"What was your weapon for?"

Kari looked down.

"I specialize in building and controlling b-bombs..." She whispered.

"But!" She cried, quickly looking up.

"Papa said I wouldn't have to hurt anyone with them, just..." She paused.

"Just what...?" Tammy asked cautiously.

Kari slowly lifted her head.

"Kaboom..." She whispered.

48 Key

"Do you mean this building is going to explode!?" Keren cried out.

Kari began tearing up again.

"I-is there any way you can defuse the bombs...?" Sena questioned.

Kari shook her head.

"W-we still have a few hours..."

Tammy looked at Kari.

"Will you at least comply with us?" She asked.

Kari made eye contact with Tammy, then quickly looked down.

"Papa won't be happy..."

Tammy suddenly grabbed her by the shoulders.

"Do you want to continue making him happy for only a few hours longer, or do you want to live!?" She shouted.

"Tammy..." Abbey whispered, stunned.

Kari looked at her and then nodded.

"Come with me...to the control room." She said.

As they quickly hurried to the control room, Abbey stopped.

"What's the matter, Abbey...?" Sena suddenly stopped as well.

"Tammy, Kari, you two go ahead," Abbey said.

"I have a bad feeling..."

The two nodded their heads as they continued running.

"What's the bad feeling?" Keren questioned.

Just as she said that, the room began shaking.

"Oh, holy shit!"

The monitor on the wall clicked on.

"Hello, intruders..." Janine's face appeared on the screen.

"That's...!" Keren turned to the other two.

"Tch..." Abbey clicked her tongue.

"We can't take her on in a physical fight..."

Janine closed her eyes, smiling.

"Exactly!" She then grinned.

"Now then..." She began.

"Today's forecast includes an artificial earthquake, with a one hundred percent chance of death!"

Just as she said that, the monitor clicked off.

The room began to shake even harder as the floor started crumbling.

Keren stumbled backward.

"Keren!" Sena and Abbey cried.

As she began to fall, a hand reached out quickly.

"Yeesh..." a voice muttered.

Keren opened her eyes, greeted by a familiar face.

"N-Norio..." She whispered.

He smiled softly as he pulled her back up.

"C'mon, we need to get out of here." He said.

They ran out of the room just as it collapsed.

*

As Kari and Tammy arrived outside the control room, they heard Janine slam her hands on the desk.

"Damnit!" She growled.

"Looks like she won't be so on board with us after all..." Tammy whispered.

"Are you sure you can't defuse them manually...?" She asked.

Kari shook her head.

"I know that I said there's not away..." She paused.

"But I panicked; it has to be by Janine's computer..."

The door quickly opened as Janine stepped out into the doorway.

 "Kari, what are you..." She looked at Tammy, then back at Kari.

"Don't tell me..." she whispered.

"Big sis, I can explain!" She cried out.

"But for now, we really need your password to defuse the bombs!" She pleaded desperately.

Janine narrowed her eyes.

"You may be a traitor...but I for one am not," Janine said as the control room door clicked shut behind her.

"Please, big sis..." Kari said as tears streamed down her face.

"You want the key?" Janine asked, glaring.

"Please!" Kari desperately pleaded.

"Please don't...!"

But it was too late; Janine chucked the keys over the balcony.

Tammy's eyes widened.

"Big sis!" Kari screamed.

Janine narrowed her eyes, letting out a sigh as she turned to walk away.

49 Final Boss

As Janine walked back to where Larkin was, she stopped for a moment.

"Was that foolish of me..." She whispered to herself.

Just as she was about to take a step forward, she bumped into Larkin.

She looked up at him, startled.

"B-boss..."

Larkin looked at her, then sighed.

"I suppose this means you weren't successful either."

Janine slowly nodded her head.

"The synchronization is near completion anyway." He said.

As he began to walk away, he turned his head.

"Don't worry about it." He said, giving a smile.

Janine's eyes widened.

"B-boss...!"

However, Larkin had already walked away.

*

Everyone had gathered around in the room where Rick, Iris Azalea, Mikael, and Chris were waiting.

"Well..." Mikael said, slowly lifting his head.

"This is it." Abbey folded her arms.

"What do you mean...?" Keren asked.

"Behind this door lies Larkin." Iris Azalea said.

The room went quiet.

"Now what..." Norio whispered.

Kari looked around the room and then at Tammy.

"We have an hour and a half..."

Rick looked up.

"Until what...?"

Kari looked at him, then quickly back down.

Tammy let out a sigh.

"Her job was to plant a few bombs to make this building blow up..."

Rick's eyes widened.

"Were you going to tell us sooner, or were we just supposed to blow up!?" He cried out.

"I have to get Maru and get the hell out of here!" He exclaimed, quickly rising.

"Rick!" Mikael shouted.

Rick quickly spun around.

"You're nowhere near ready to take him on!"

Rick's eyes widened.

"Do you mean..."

Mikael looked down.

"By now, the power transfer should have been a success..."

Rick huffed.

"I don't give a crap!" He began.

"Maru is still in there; like hell I'll let that bastard take another thing from me!" He screamed as he ran to the door.

"Open this damn door!" He growled as he began pounding on it with his fists.

Mikael looked at him, then sighed.

"I suppose we really don't have time to waste..."

Keren looked at Norio.

"I'll do anything to see that bright smile of hers again, Nori..." She whispered.

Norio looked at her and then stood up.

"I'm going with you..." He said.

Mikael let out a nervous chuckle.

"Well, whether we want to go or not, we don't have a choice..."

Kari looked up.

"The door is a trap; if someone stays behind without the key, they'll get left behind in the explosion."

Rick let out a huff.

"Mikael, open this damn door already!"

Mikael looked at him, then gave a sad smile.

"On the count of three, we all run in there," he paused.

"There's no guarantee if any of us will make it out alive..."

Everyone glanced around the room.

Sena reached for Abbey's hand.

Abbey gently stroked her hand and smiled at her sadly.

"One." Everyone got up, Norio helping Chris up.

"Two." Everyone readied themselves.

"Three...!" The door slowly began to open, revealing on the other side Larkin, Mim, and Janine.

Larkin stood on the balcony next to the tubes, grinning.

"Now!" Mikael cried.

Rick led the charge as everyone hurried out of the room.

The solid door closed, locking tightly.

"To the final boss..." Mikael whispered.

50 Own Way

As they entered, Larkin chuckled.

"How amusing..." He said, looking at Rick.

"So, you've decided to abandon the mask, eh, Mr. Reaper?" He grinned.

"Larkin!" Rick screamed.

"I'm afraid that you're already too late; the synchronization was a success." He knocked on the tubes.

"Alas, despite your status as a notorious killer, I'm afraid you'll be beaten to a pulp within a mere few seconds."

Rick growled.

"However, perhaps your friends may be able to take on my underlings while you warm up." He said, leaning on the balcony.

Rick quickly turned to the group.

"I have a grudge with the pink bastard." Norio sighed as he took a step forward.

"Did you see how Chris ended up!?" Rick cried.

"Forget it; he's just taunting you!"

Suddenly, Mim appeared behind Norio.

"A grudge with little old me?" He asked.

"How amusing..."

Norio quickly spun around.

"That is," he began.

"If you're fast enough!" He cried as he went to kick his leg.

Norio quickly dodged. Panting, he put up his fists.

"Nori, you better be careful!" Keren cried out.

Norio examined the room.

His eye widened as Mim quickly came from behind him. Norio quickly ducked.

"This is lame." Mim huffed.

"Are you going to try offense soon or what?" Mim asked.

Norio lifted his leg, kicking in a circle.

"Tch!" Mim appeared as he fell to the ground.

"I didn't mean right this second!" He cried.

That's it; when he's immobile on the ground, he's vulnerable! Norio thought to himself.

He quickly began kicking.

Mim grinned as each kick hit.

He then grabbed Norio's leg.

However, Norio kicked him with his other leg and spun out from the lock.

"Shit!" Mim grunted as Norio continuously kicked him.

"The hell are you so quiet for, you-"

Norio kicked him in the mouth before he could finish.

"I'm not here to play, dumbass!" He growled.

"My kids' life is not a game!" He shouted as he kicked the final blow.

Everyone watched on, stunned.

However, Larkin chuckled in amusement.

"You've grown, Norio."

Norio quickly looked up.

His eye widened.

*

"Why did you think a knife fight with an eleven-year-old was a good idea!?" Mikael cried out.

Larkin was silent.

Norio nervously hovered in the doorway; the two adults unaware.

"Don't you think these children need self-defense?" Larkin finally spoke.

"Yes, but!" Mikael paused as he looked at Larkin as he chuckled.

"What is so funny?" He glared.

"Nothing, it's just, Rick has shown potential, is all," Larkin said.

"Potential for what!?" Mikael angrily snapped.

"Oh, it's nothing..." Larkin sighed.

Mikael looked down.

"Larkin, don't tell me..."

Larkin chuckled.

"You worry too much, Mikael." He said, patting him on the shoulder.

He then frowned.

"You know, on the other hand," he paused.

"Norio is far too weak..."

Norio's eyes widened.

"Do you think he'll be able to protect anyone the way he is...?"

Mikael was silent.

"Tell me?" Larkin asked.

"He has a good heart; he will protect what he needs to, in his own way," Mikael said, giving a big smile.

"I believe in him."

Larkin looked at him, then let out a sigh.

"Have it your way..."

Norio then came out of hiding, tearing up, causing the two adults to panic quickly.

*

"That day..." Norio said, turning to Mikael.

Mikael quickly looked up.

"Have I grown stronger...to protect what I want in my own way?"

Mikael looked down as he smiled.

"Ah, you've grown into a fine young man, able to protect what's dear to him in your own special way."

Norio looked at him, then smiled.

"Thank you for believing in me..."

Mikael closed his eyes.

"Fight for what you believe in, always."

Norio nodded.

"Norio..." Rick whispered.

Larkin closed his eyes, smiling.

"Rick." He began.

Rick quickly turned his head.

Larkin quickly jumped from the balcony, lunging at Rick.

51 Familiar

Rick's eyes widened as Larkin lunged at him, quickly he ducked.

Larkin began to throw punches, Rick dodging as if his life depended on it.

"Why are you doing this!?" Mikael cried.

Rick quickly turned his head, just as Larkin threw a punch, hitting Rick in his abdomen.

Rick let out a wheeze as he fell to the ground.

Larkin smirked, grabbing Rick by his face.

He tossed Rick up in the air, as if he were a rag doll, then pinned him by his head against the wall.

"Rick!" Norio screamed.

Mikael began running; suddenly, Janine grabbed his cloak.

"Do you see how dangerous he is!?" She cried.

Mim sat up, groaning.

"She's right...the boss is incredibly dangerous, at this point..." He looked up at Rick and Larkin.

"Forget it...he's dead."

All anyone could do was simply watch.

Rick's eyes darted towards the tubes containing Maru and Emersyn.

Larkin then squeezed his head.

Rick grunted in pain.

"Oi," Larkin spoke.

"Look at me." Larkin took his fingers to pry open Rick's eye manually.

Larkin gave a unique grin, all too familiar to Rick.

*

"Rick," Larkin began, rising from the kitchen table.

Rick turned to look at him.

"Meet me outside."

*

As Rick stepped outside, he ran over to Larkin.

"What's up?" He asked.

"I want to entrust you with something." He said, fishing in his pants pocket.

"Really!?" Rick asked eagerly.

"Ah, got it," Larkin said.

"Hold out your hands and close your eyes."

Rick happily cooperated.

"Open," Larkin said.

As Rick opened his eyes, he looked down to see a pocket knife.

"Oh..." He whispered.

"You don't like it?" Larkin frowned, kneeling.

"N-no...!" Rick smiled sheepishly.

"I just don't know what it is..." He admitted.

"Ah." Larkin smiled.

"Well, it's a pocket knife." He said, ruffling Rick's hair.

Rick stared down at the knife.

"Does it cut food...?" He asked.

Larkin closed his eyes, smiling.

"Not quite..." He chuckled.

"Why don't I demonstrate to you just what it does?"
He said, rising.

Rick looked up at him.

"Ok!" He said, running over to him.

Larkin flipped out another pocketknife.

"Go stand back over there," Larkin instructed.

Rick hurriedly ran back.

"Flip the knife out."

Rick looked at the knife in confusion.

"H-how...?"

Larkin clicked his tongue.

"Hold on..." He said, walking over.

"Like this." He said, showing him.

"Oh!" Rick nodded.

"Are you just saying you know, or do you know?"

Rick puffed his cheeks in annoyance.

"I know!" He protested.

"Fine, prove it to me."

Rick, with ease, flipped the knife open.

"Ah..." Larkin smiled.

"Now, I'll go over there." He said, walking away.

"Now," Larkin began.

"Straighten up." Rick quickly straightened up.

"That's...too straight." Larkin chuckled.

"Relax more."

Rick stuck his tongue out and then tried to relax.

"Perfect..." Larkin smiled.

"Now, get ready..."

Rick, looking down at the knife, quickly picked his head up.

Just as he did, Larkin came charging at him.

A sinister grin spread across his face;one that Rick would never be able to get out of his head.

Rick's eyes widened as Larkin raised his knife.

Rick barely dodged as the knife cut through his sleeve and sliced a tiny bit of his arm.

Rick fell to the ground.

He grabbed his now bleeding arm; tears began to well in his eyes.

He then began crying hysterically.

"Oi..." Larkin said, waving his hands to get him to quiet down.

"C-come on..." He whispered, picking Rick up.

"It barely touched you..." Rick sobbed into Larkin's shoulder.

Larkin sighed as he began to walk back toward the house.

"Mikael is going to kill me..." He sighed, rubbing Rick's back.

*

Rick gasped for air, but Larkin's grip was suffocating.

Larkin proceeded to squeeze even tighter.

"W-why are you..." Rick whispered as everything faded to black.

52 Promises

"Rick!" A voice cried out.

"Rick!" The voice shouted once again.

Rick's eyes flickered. He grunted, rubbing his head as he sat up.

When he opened his eyes, he gasped, scooting backward.

Kneeling in front of him was Cole.

"W-What are you..." He whispered.

Then the realization set in.

"Am I...?"

Cole smiled.

"Please don't worry; you're only unconscious."

Rick looked at him, then let out a sigh of relief.

"Is this real...are you...?"

He extended his hand, patting Cole on the head.

Cole giggled.

"What are you doing here..."

Cole closed his eyes, smiling.

"I'm here to thank you finally!" He said, beaming.

"For what...?" Rick asked as he stroked Cole's head.

"Thank you for keeping our promise." He said.

Rick looked down.

"What's wrong?" Cole asked.

"Maru is..."

Cole began laughing.

Rick quickly looked up.

"Maru is safe, Rick."

Rick's eyes widened.

Tears began welling in his eyes. He looked down as tears streamed down his face.

"I'm sorry..."

Cole cocked his head.

"For what?" He asked.

Rick looked up. He slowly lifted a hand, touching Cole's cheek.

"Because of me, you're..." He stroked Cole's cheek gently.

Cole kept smiling.

"Because of you, I'm free..."

Rick looked up at him.

"Because of you, Maru is free." He said, tears in his eyes.

"Your job isn't finished yet, though!" He exclaimed, wrapping his arms around Rick.

As he whispered something into Rick's ear, Rick smiled.

"Promise?" Cole asked, smiling as he faded.

*

Rick's eyes widened as he regained consciousness. He breathed heavily.

As he looked over at Larkin, he noticed his shocked expression.

However, Larkin wasn't paying attention to Rick, but rather the others.

Rick weakly turned his head to see what was going on. All he could make out was muffled screaming.

"Now's my chance..." He whispered.

He weakly stood up. Larkin was still too absorbed with the others.

Rick grabbed the sword. He breathed heavily as he held the sword in his hand.

He remembered the knife match years ago. He closed his eyes, gripping the sword.

Just as Larkin turned around, Rick was coming at him.

"Larkin!" Rick screamed as he jumped in the air.

Larkin's eyes widened. As he saw Rick coming at him, he also saw the child he had let down. The boy he had cut so deeply.

Rick let out a cry as he came flying to the ground.

There was a long, suffocating moment of silence.

Larkin opened his eyes.

They widened as he saw the sword, as well as Rick just inches away from him.

Rick was huffing and panting heavily.

"You..." Larkin whispered.

"I can't bring myself to do it..." Rick whispered, smiling.

"I promised..." He said, tearing up.

53 Larkin

A man whistled as he was walking through the woods.

"Finally." He stopped, staring at a building.

"I made it." He spoke into a watch.

"Burn it." A voice from the other end as instructed.

"Roger." The man said, clicking the watch off.

The man stared at the building for a second. He shook his head as he made his way towards the building.

Suddenly, two little boys ran past him, one accidentally bumping into him.

"Oh, sorry, mister!" One boy said, grabbing the other boy.

The man gave a stern look.

"It's dangerous around these parts; you kids should go home." The man spoke.

The boys looked up at him.

"Fine..." The boy huffed and then quickly turned his head to the other boy.

"Let's play just one more round, baby bro!" The older boy said.

"Mm!" The younger boy cheerfully replied.

The older boy grabbed the younger boy's hand, and the two ran off.

The man watched and then let out a sigh.

*

The man followed through with his mission, setting the building ablaze.

"The mission was a success... the Sunshine orphanage is burning nicely..." He spoke into the watch.

"Excellent, return." The watch clicked off.

As he turned to leave, he saw the two boys from earlier.

The boy's eyes wide with fear, watching their home burning.

"Rick..." The younger boy whimpered.

Rick quickly turned his attention back to the other boy.

"N-Nori, it's ok...!" He said, pressing the boys to head to his chest.

The boys then noticed the man.

Rick's eyes widened. "Did you..." He whispered.

The man looked at the boys. There was silence for a moment before the man spoke up.

"I told you it wasn't safe around here..." He said as he walked past them.

Norio began sobbing.

The man suddenly stopped. He looked at the boys momentarily, then let out a sigh.

"There's an abandoned cottage nearby...follow me."

Rick looked down at Norio.

"How do we know you're not lying..."

The man then began to laugh.

 "I promise."

Rick's eyes widened upon hearing those words.

*

"Are we there yet...?" Rick whined.

"Just a little further." The man said.

Norio held onto Rick's hand as he was curiously looking around the forest.

"Ah, there it is." The man said, pointing.

"By the way, mister..." Rick began.

The man turned his head.

"What's your name...?" He asked.

The man looked at him, and then closed his eyes.

"You can call me Larkin." The man said, smiling.

54 Mikael

As they arrived at the cabin, Norio let out a yawn.

Larkin turned to him.

"Are you tired?"

Norio nodded.

"I'm sure it's been a long day." Larkin smiled.

"What do we do now?" Rick looked up at Larkin.

"What do you mean?" Larkin asked.

"We need food..."

Norio's stomach began to rumble.

"Sorry..." He said, shyly holding his stomach.

Larkin sat on a chair and let out a sigh.

"There's a village down the hill..."

Rick looked at him.

"What's that look for?" Larkin asked.

"We're too tired, right, Nori?"

Norio nodded.

"Too tired!" He repeated.

Larkin let out a sigh.

"Fine, I guess I'll have to go by myself then."

Rick folded his arms, nodding.

"Looks like we have no other choice!"

Larkin's eye twitched in annoyance.

*

As Larkin headed out, he scratched his head.

"I'm not obligated to return..." He whispered.

"Then again..." He began to think about the fact that without him, the boys would most likely end up dead one way or another.

Larkin let out a sigh of frustration.

"Fine, guess I have no choice!" He grumbled angrily.

"Oi," a voice called out.

Larkin quickly spun around.

"What the hell are you doing?" A man asked, leaning on a tree.

Larkin narrowed his eyes, studying the man.

"Do I... know you?" He asked.

"Hah!?" The man cried.

"We've been working together for months now...!" He cried.

"Anyway..." He coughed.

"The name's Mikael." He said.

Larkin shook his head.

"Doesn't ring a bell..." He whispered.

"Not the point!" Mikael cried.

"What the hell are you doing out here!?"

Larkin looked up.

"I..." He looked around.

"P-picking berries..."

Mikael folded his arms.

"Oh, really, where are they then?"

Larkin blushed.

"I ate them..." He mumbled.

Mikael shot him a look.

"You are such a liar!" He cried.

"Ok, ok, look..." Larkin waved his hands.

"The truth is..." He looked around.

"There were two boys outside playing when I burned the orphanage down."

Mikael quickly looked up.

"And now because of me, they have nowhere to go..." He whispered.

"Larkin..." Mikael whispered.

He then smirked.

"Didn't think you'd have a soft spot."

Larkin blushed.

"I-it's not like that...!" He cried.

"In truth...I don't know what to do; I can't let them starve..."

Mikael then pointed.

"There's a village down this hill."

Larkin looked at him.

"Yeah, no shit."

Mikael puffed his cheeks in annoyance.

"Listen, just...tell the organization I died or something," Larkin said, looking down.

Mikael looked at him, and he then sighed.

"I can't."

Larkin let out a sigh.

"Because I want to help too!" He beamed.

Larkin looked at him.

"Did you eat poisonous berries or something, or are you just insane?"

Mikael grinned.

"I have a weak spot for kids, and honestly, this job drains me, and besides," he paused.

"It can be our little secret!" He beamed.

Larkin looked at him, then laughed.

"So, you really are insane..." He said as he closed his eyes, smiling.

"Come on; they're starving and cranky..." Larkin said as he began walking toward the village.

"Mm!" Mikael nodded, running to catch up with him.

55 Explosion

"What kind of killer lets his victims go..."

Rick began as he looked at Larkin.

"You and I... are the same." He whispered, with a sad smile on his face.

Larkin stared at him.

"The bombs are going to detonate in fifteen minutes!" Kari cried.

Larkin's eyes widened.

"Where's the key?" He asked.

Janine looked down in shame.

"We can't find it and don't have time to go and search for it!" Kari shouted.

Larkin turned to face Rick.

"We don't have time; go get your child, and leave."

He turned to Norio.

"Get up here; we don't have time!" He shouted.

Norio quickly began running up.

"What the hell is this glass made of!?" Rick grumbled.

"Larkin, do you have a code?" Norio questioned.

Larkin scratched his head.

"I don't remember..." He sighed.

"Rick!" Abbey shouted, tossing her sword at him.

Rick caught it and turned to the tube.

"Maru..." He whispered.

"Hurry!" Norio cried.

Rick pierced the tube with the sword, causing the liquid to spill.

He grabbed Maru.

"Please hold her for a sec." He said, handing her to Larkin.

Larkin looked at the girl in his arms, smiling sadly.

"I'm sorry..." He whispered.

"Eight minutes!" Kari shouted.

Rick quickly pierced through Emersyn's tube.

Norio gently grabbed the unconscious girl.

"Six!"

Larkin handed Maru back to Rick.

"I'll activate a barrier..." He then turned to Rick.

"At this rate, you won't be able to make it very far; the barrier will protect you and everyone else from the explosion."

Rick's eyes widened.

Larkin gave a sad smile.

"Rick," he began.

"Please, hurry!" Sena cried.

"Four!"

Janine and Mim walked up to Larkin.

"Boss, we won't let you go alone..."

Mim smiled.

"Are you two nuts!?" Larkin cried.

"We contributed to this mess..." Janine whispered.

"Oi, bandages, glasses," Mim began.

"Run like hell."

Rick's eyes widened.

"But!"

Norio grabbed his hand and started running.

"The barrier is activated..." Larkin smiled, sitting down.

Mim and Janine sat on either side of him, putting their arms around him.

"What are they..." Chris whispered.

"We don't have time to figure it out!" Abbey cried, grabbing him.

"Papa!" Kari cried.

Larkin looked at her, smiling.

"You've grown into a fine young girl..." He whispered.

Tammy grabbed Kari's arm and began to run.

"That goes for all of you..." He closed his eyes.

"Thank you..." He whispered.

As everyone else quickly filled the barrier, they turned back to the building.

"L-" Rick's eyes widened.

The bombs then detonated.

"LARKIN!" Rick screamed at the top of his lungs.

56 Exchange

Nobody had spoken a word on their walk back to town.

"Our house is this way..." Mikael said, breaking the silence.

"I suggest taking Maru and Emersyn to the hospital immediately."

Rick nodded his head.

"I'll try to visit when I can..." Mikael gave a sad smile.

"I'm just glad they're safe..." He said, patting an unconscious Maru's head.

"C'mon, Iris Azalea." Mikael stretched as he yawned.

"Mm." She nodded.

"See you." She said as she waved goodbye to the group.

*

As they arrived at the hospital, Vera and Norio's sister were seated in the waiting room.

Norio handed Emersyn to Keren.

Hiromi lightly shook a sleeping Vera.

Vera sleepily opened her eyes, looking up.

Her eyes widened as she saw Norio, immediately standing up to hug him.

She began crying. Norio rubbed her back. He gave a sad smile.

"Hey, Norio," Keren began, then noticed he was tearing up.

"No way..." She whispered.

Norio knelt, hugging Vera, as he broke down sobbing.

Vera stroked his head as they both cried.

Keren began tearing up at the sight.

 "Hey."

She quickly turned around to Hiromi.

"How is she...?"

Keren looked down at an unconscious Emersyn.

"She's...safe, at least." Keren smiled.

Hiromi nodded.

"Thank goodness..." She whispered.

*

There were screams of pain coming from inside the hospital room.

"Well, her arms have a broken sensation." The doctor informed Rick.

"However, strangely enough, on the outside, they appear normal," he paused.

"They will also heal within a week or so..."

Rick nodded.

"Thank you," he said as the door shut.

Rick turned to Maru, who had finally calmed down.

"Hey..." He whispered.

Maru looked at him.

He knelt, smiling.

"You're so brave, kiddo..." He whispered, stroking her head.

"I love you..." He said as tears filled his eyes.

He kissed the top of her head as he continued running his fingers through her hair.

"I love you..." She whispered back.

"Oi," the door opened.

Rick turned around to see Norio in the doorway.

"Y-Yeah?" He looked up.

"Have a minute?" He asked.

"S-sure." Rick stood up, patting Maru's head.

"Mikael went to the aftermath to see if he could collect anything...for the wake."

Rick looked steadily down.

"He wanted to know if you wanted to attend...it'd be just us."

Rick looked at him.

"Who's us?"

Norio looked down.

"Our family."

Rick kept his gaze down.

"Sure." He nodded.

"By the way..." Norio cleared his throat.

"C-can we exchange numbers?" He paused.

"J-just so I can text you about the preparations..."

Rick looked up at him and couldn't help but laugh.

Norio blushed.

"Don't be such a stranger, you jerk..." He chuckled.

Norio looked up at him.

"Brothers...?" He asked, extending his hand.

Rick looked at him, then smiled.

"Of course!" He said, shaking his hand firmly.

Norio began to laugh.

Rick couldn't help but laugh, too.

"Looks like this is the closest they've been in years..." Sena whispered, smiling.

Keren nodded.

"If anything, good came out of all of this mess; it's this..." She smiled.

"I've never seen him so happy..." Keren whispered.

57 Cheers

As Rick stepped outside of his house, he let out a sigh.

"Today's going to be a long day..." He grumbled.

"Are you okay?" Chris asked.

"Yeah, are you sure you're ok with watching Maru today...?"

Chris gave a smile.

"Of course, I am."

Rick smiled.

"Thanks." He said.

"Oi!" Norio called out, riding upon his moped.

"Eh!?" Rick cried.

Norio gave him a look.

"Hop on." He said.

*

"How'd you learn how to drive?" Rick questioned.

"My mother," Norio replied.

"Do you mean..."

As they stopped at a stoplight, Norio sighed.

"Guess we have a lot of catching up to do, huh?" He smiled.

Rick laughed.

*

"Oh, there you are," Mikael said, getting up from a seat.

"Yeah, sorry, we kind of hit a lot of lights..." Rick chuckled, scratching his head.

"This way," Mikael pointed to a room.

"Oh, so it is just us here..." Rick whispered, sticking his head in the room.

Iris Azalea looked up.

"Hello." She waved.

"Closed casket?" Rick whispered, kneeling at the altar.

"While I'm sure you're used to the gore, I'm not sure the other two are," Mikael whispered.

Rick stared steadily at the coffin.

"Mikael..." He began.

Mikael leaned down, patting his back.

"What's up?"

Rick stared down at the coffin.

"Hate to say this at his wake, but..." He looked up at Mikael.

"I don't know if I'll ever fully forgive him."

Mikael closed his eyes, nodding.

"Listen, Rick," he began.

"There are days where I feel bitter about his actions and what he did to us," he paused.

"Guess I really can't help but love the man I should hate..." He said, with tears in his eyes.

"Mikael..." Rick whispered, leaning his head on him.

*

"The burial will take place tomorrow at Saint Joseph's cemetery," Mikael informed Norio and Rick.

"Got it." Norio nodded.

"I'll pick you up tomorrow then." He said, turning to Rick.

"Thanks," Rick said.

"Can I offer you boys drinks on me?" Mikael smiled.

"I think we need them."

The two looked at each other.

"I don't know...Maru's at home and-" He paused as Mikael gave him a look.

"Just stay over at our place," he smiled.

Iris Azalea looked at him.

"F-Fine..." Rick chuckled.

*

The men clinked their glasses together.

"Cheers to family." Mikael toasted with a smile.

"To family." The boys repeated as they took a shot.

58 This Promise

"Are you sure you don't need any kind of medicine for your hangover?" Mikael chuckled.

"Nah, I'm good, but thanks," Rick said, letting out a groan.

"See you at the cemetery." Iris Azalea said as she shut the door.

"I didn't think you'd be such a lightweight, big bro," Norio smirked.

"Shut it," Rick grumbled as he put his helmet on.

*

As they arrived back at Rick's place, Rick hopped off the moped.

"Thanks for the lift." He said.

"Take good care of your girls and Keren; I'll talk to you later." He smiled.

"Ah, same goes for you." He smiled.

He then gave a wave as he drove off.

Rick smiled, watching him go.

*

"Rick!" Maru cried as he entered the house.

She quickly ran over to hug him.

"Hey, kiddo!" Rick said, kneeling to pet her head.

"Hey!" Chris greeted.

"Did the funeral take place already...?" He asked.

Rick shook his head.

"Later in the day," he said.

"Anyways," Rick began.

"Thank you for watching her."

Chris chuckled.

"Of course, man, it's the least I can do." He said, smiling.

Rick smiled.

"Any news from Sena or Abbey?" Rick asked.

"Well, Kari has been down in the dumps, so they, along with Tammy, took her on a shopping spree."

Rick nodded.

"I hope her living there now is not too much of a burden to place on them..." He whispered.

Chris shrugged.

"They seemed happy to take her in." He said.

"Anyways, I have to get going," Chris said as he yawned.

"Understandable, Maru, come, and say goodbye to Chris."

Maru ran over to Chris, hugging him.

"I love you, Chris!" She beamed.

Chris laughed.

"Love you too, shrimp." He said, ruffling her hair.

"Well, I'll talk to you later." Chris waved as he walked out.

*

"Oi, Maru," Rick began, sitting on the couch.

"Mm?" Maru said, plopping down.

"Do you want to come to visit Cole with me today?"

Maru looked at him, then nodded.

"Mm!" She smiled.

"Sena said we could take a few flowers..." Rick said, looking down at his phone.

"Do you want to pick some out?" He turned to Maru.

"Mm!" She nodded, looking around Sena's shop.

"These orange ones!" She cried, pointing.

Rick looked over.

"Was that his favorite color?" He asked.

Maru nodded her head.

"Quit nodding so fast; you'll give yourself a headache." He smiled, patting her head.

*

"I'm pretty sure it's this way..." Rick said.

Maru hopped along beside him.

"What are you doing?" He chuckled, looking over.

"I can't step on a crack!" She cried.

Rick laughed.

As they arrived, Rick's eyes widened.

Annette was sitting in front of Cole's grave.

She turned her head.

"Oh, Rick." She said.

"H-hey, Annette...!" He laughed nervously.

"I was just about to leave..." She said, getting up.

"Rick," she said, closing her eyes.

"Thank you for keeping your promise to Cole..." She smiled as she began walking away.

 "Oh." She stopped.

"Take care, Maru." She waved before turning around and leaving.

Rick looked down at Maru, who had grabbed his hand.

He smiled as he stroked her hand.

*

"Ok, place them in the water..." He instructed her.

"Got it!" Maru said, placing the flowers down.

"Good job." Rick smiled, giving her a high five.

The wind suddenly began blowing strong.

"Guess he really liked these flowers..." Rick whispered, smiling.

*

As Rick arrived home from the funeral, he opened his bedroom door.

As he turned on the lights, he noticed a sleeping Maru.

"Ah..." He whispered.

Maru's eyes flickered.

"Don't worry, kiddo, it's just me..." He smiled, climbing in.

Maru smiled at him, giving a sleepy nod.

As he lay in bed, running his fingers through Maru's hair, he couldn't help but smile.

"Cole..." He whispered.

"Turns out our promise is a lifelong commitment..." He said as he closed his eyes.

"That's ok...I don't mind." He mumbled.

"A promise is a promise after all..." He smiled.

"This promise..." He whispered.

"I don't mind keeping it..." He closed his eyes, kissing Maru's head.

"I love you, Maru..." He whispered as he drifted off to sleep.

About the Author

JJ Dizz is the author of 246. They have a passion for character creating. JJ Dizz has always aspired to become an author, writing dozens of drafts since their youth.

Author's Contact

Email - teamrocketcutie@aol.com

Twitter – JJ_Dizz

Tumblr - teamrocketcutie

Deviantart - shimura-shinpachi

Webnovel - JD246

Main Instagram - jj_desantis

Art Instagram - jd246_

Facebook – JJ DeSantis

246 Discord server - https://discordapp.com/invite/aj7A6g6

Paypal - paypal.me/teamrocketcutie

CPSIA information can be obtained
at www.ICGtesting.com
Printed in the USA
BVHW090206290721
613076BV00022B/1511